© 20

Author's Note

Thank you for joining me for my first adventure on the Enchanted Coast! This book was a ton of fun to write, and I'll be following up with Book 2, The Surfboard Slaying, soon. These books are a little lighter than my other series; my goal was to create a quick, light read great for an afternoon at home, or to bring some magic to your own Enchanted Coast vacation.
Enjoy!

CHAPTER ONE

"Stan, what have I told you about bringing the Cupid's bow into the bar? And adjust your diaper. None of us want to see what's under that."

I heaved a sigh of exasperation. I loved my job, but sometimes I felt more like a babysitter at a daycare center than a cocktail waitress at a magical beach resort.

He scowled as he reached for his margarita. "It's a loincloth. And what do you want me to do—leave my bow and arrows in my room? They won't fit in the safe."

Cyri, the faerie sitting one table over, turned to look at him. "That's easy enough to fix," she said, adjusting her lavender ponytail. She dipped her finger into a waterproof pouch hanging from the pink lanyard around her neck, then sprinkled a small pinch of sparkling dust over the bow and quiver.

Stan watched in fascinated horror as the tool of his trade shrunk to a tenth of its size. "You can't just do that," he said, indignant. "What if I get called out to a job?"

She snorted. "That's like your fourth margarita. You're in no condition to fly, anyway. And I've only been with Aiden a few months. It would be a disaster if he accidentally nicked himself with one of those arrows on his way to the bathroom. I'm not ready for the whole L-word scenario."

I smiled as I walked away. Stan was in the middle of an existential crisis. His problem was that he was a romantic at heart, and his job wasn't just a job to him—it was his passion. Between the free-love movement and easy, DIY divorces, he was having a hard time believing he hadn't outlived his purpose.

So, he was on an extended vacation to find himself and decide whether or not he should retire. But just because I felt sorry for the guy didn't mean I could give him a pass on the bow. Can you imagine how the *I love you, man* phase of intoxication works when a cupid wants to make the whole bar happy at closing time? Yeah, no love-laced arrows allowed.

I delivered the last drinks on my tray to a group of sunbathing selkies that were regulars, thinking how hot their seal-skin beach blankets must be. Before you get upset about animal cruelty, selkies are seals in the water but shed their skins to become human on land.

I couldn't blame them for keeping them secure though. Julius, their leader, had left his skin unattended at the bar when he'd gone to the bathroom a few years ago, and we'd had to lock down the whole resort for a couple hours.

A beach attendant had mistakenly picked it up and thrown it into the laundry, and since I'd been the one to call for the lockdown *and* the one to find it, he'd granted me honorary membership in his pod. In short, when they came every few months, they requested me, and they always tipped generously. It was job security, but it made me feel good, too.

Angie, Julius's wife, passed the martinis down the row, taking a sip from the last one.

"Divine as always," she said, licking the vodka mustache off her upper lip. "Tell Bob he used just the right amount of anchovy juice."

I bit back a shudder at the phantom flavor and assured her I would. As I picked my way through the tables back to the shade of the tiki bar, I picked up a few more drink orders along the way.

Plunking my tray down on the server's deck at the bar, I leaned over and rested my chin in my hand while I waited for Bob, the Bigfoot bartender, to finish telling a joke to a broody werewolf. I don't know why he bothered—the guy hadn't cracked a smile the whole week he'd been there. He'd eaten his weight in steak and was a fat tipper, though, so I guess Bob felt obligated.

The big lug tended to be a people-pleaser anyway, so the more somebody rejected his efforts, the harder he tried. That alone kinda made me want to crack the shifter with my tray for being such a buzzkill.

I shifted over a couple feet and turned a fan so it was blowing in my face. The heat was brutal, and there hadn't been a mermaid or water nymph around all day. I liked it when they came, because it gave me an excuse to wade out to the water bar to wait on them—a definite plus when the thermometer pushed past ninety.

We also had a huge salt-chlorinated, zero-entry infinity pool that had a direct-connect to the ocean, so it was available to everybody. Unfortunately, it was closed for cleaning; a group of unicorns had their son's birthday party in there the day before and ... kids were kids. So, no wading around the edges to deliver drinks. The fan would have to do.

Bob lumbered over to pick up my drink ticket. "Man, that guy's tough," he whispered. "I'm throwin' my best material at him, and *nothing*. I can't get him to look away from that laptop."

I tilted my head and examined the guy in question as he stared at the screen like it held the secrets to the universe. Good-looking, as most werewolves were, but he lacked the lightheartedness that marked most of his kind.

"What's his deal, anyway?"

"No idea," Bob said, muddling mint and simple syrup for a mojito. "He's met with Cass a couple times, but that's it. And every time he has, his mood's seemed worse."

That wasn't an atypical response to dealing with our boss though, so it didn't add anything to the speculation. It would have been more unusual had he come away smiling.

Speaking of ...

"Maganti!" Somebody bellowed my last name from behind me.

Before turning, I pulled a deep breath in through my nose and blew it out through my mouth, counting to five as I did.

My boss, Cassiel—otherwise known as the disgraced Angel of Temperance—was a blowhard and an idiot. I wasn't sure who'd assigned him to be the figurehead of that particular virtue, but apparently they hadn't been practicing it themselves when they'd made the call.

It had taken a few millennia, but he'd finally pushed his luck one too many times with the powers that be and was tossed out on his ear, much to the chagrin of everybody in the mortal realm, or at least those of us who lived on the Enchanted Coast. Managing the beach bar was his booby prize, and he lorded over it like the planet owed him a living.

As usual, he was already half in the bag, which meant he was gonna be even more horrid than he was when sober. He was the only downside to this job. Well, him and sand in awkward places, but the latter was an easy fix.

Bob finished making the last of my drinks and ambled the couple of steps back to me, a concerned expression on his heavy features as he set them down.

"Don't bait him, Destiny," he pleaded under his breath. "Just find out what he wants, do it, then ignore him. He's just looking for an excuse to can you. Again."

"He can try," I said, lifting a shoulder. He'd fired me the previous summer, for three weeks until word spread to my regulars. It seemed I had a following that had some pull with the higher-ups. Not only had I been reinstated, I'd gotten a raise. Needless to say, that hadn't gone over well with Cassiel.

Still, I loved my job, and goodwill was a fickle beast. As a people person and a water witch who didn't want to live in the closet, the Enchanted Coast—a magical vacation resort on the Gulf of Mexico designed to meet the needs of paranormals—was the best of all worlds. So, in the interest of keeping the peace, I pivoted toward him, gritting my teeth and pasting on a smile.

"Yeah, Cass?" I said, putting everything I had into being pleasant.

Not even attempting to return the courtesy, he gestured toward the outside tables. "The place is a mess. That table needs bussed, and there are empty cups everywhere. And those fans are for guests only—not lazy waitresses."

I glanced around the area and ran my tongue over my teeth. "First," I said, still trying to maintain my fragile mask of civility, "that table is occupied. They're in the water. Second, there are exactly two empty cups, both of which just blew out of the trash can when you stormed by it and flexed your wings." I decided to let the fan comment drop. "But I'll get right on it."

I had no idea what the reason was for his animosity. He'd despised me from day one, even before he had to eat crow and hire me back. I could get along with the devil himself if he was willing to meet me halfway, but despite my efforts, Cass refused to play nice.

After a while, I'd given up. The only thing I could figure was I'd been offered his job before he was sentenced to it. I'd turned it down because I would have gotten paid less to do more, after I added in my tips.

"And since you have time to stand around," he sneered, foul as always, "go clean out the unicorn pen. People can see those rainbow turds from the hotel, and the cotton-candy smell is disgusting."

Bending over to pick up the cups, I muttered an anatomically impossible suggestion for what *he* could go do.

"What was that?" he asked, narrowing his bloodshot eyes at me.

I heaved a sigh. As usual, I was gonna have to be the bigger person. "Nothin', Cass," I said, waving him off as I went for the shovel. "Just ... have another drink."

With one stroke of the ginormous ashen wings that marked him as a fallen angel, he was towering over me, swaying a little, the smell of old whiskey seeping from his pores. I straightened my spine as my magic surged. The last thing I was willing to do was give in to a bully, even if he was an angel and my boss to boot.

"Hey Cass," a centaur named Evan called from behind him. "Cut her some slack. My drink hasn't gone empty all day, and she just finished busting her ass keeping a ten-top of gorgons happy. She's earned a minute in front of the fan."

Fiona, the leader of the gorgons he was referencing, exited the bathroom in time to hear Evan's comment, patting her turban to make sure all her snakes were safely tucked away. She glided over to me and handed me an extra fifty, assessing the situation as she did so. Cass was no stranger to her, nor was he a friend.

"Thanks, sweetie. You were a doll as always," she said, giving me a faint smile along with the bill.

She peered down her nose at Cass, her lip curled in disgust. "Bitter angel. Unless you'd like a peek at my girls, I suggest you be nice."

She was talking about the ones under her turban, not the ones under her bathing-suit wrap—you know, the ones that could turn him to stone. Fascinated as everybody else was with the exchange, they turned away just in case.

"That won't be necessary," he ground out, glaring at me.

"Pity," she said, flapping a hand. "The resort could use an angel statue, and it would be my pleasure to donate one." She maintained eye contact for a couple seconds, possibly hoping he'd give her a reason, then turned and strode away.

Cass turned to me as I picked up the cups and pointed an angry, albeit shaky, finger at me. "One of these days, I'm gonna find a reason to fire you for good."

My thin veneer of respect slipped, and I spun on him, my sense of fair play offended beyond reason. I hadn't done anything to deserve his attitude.

"Yeah," I said, shoving the cups down in the can with more force than was necessary, "and one of these days, my fairy godmother's gonna grant my wish and you'll drop dead for good. But until one of those days arrives, I guess we're stuck with each other."

It wasn't even an hour later that I regretted those words. Not because I suddenly developed a case of the warm-and-fuzzies for him, but because I was the prime suspect in his murder.

CHAPTER TWO

AFTER MAKING HIMSELF a Jack and water, Cass strode past the werewolf as if he didn't know him and out to a waterside table where two of his minions, a couple of shady-looking gargoyles, were sitting.

Amber and Dax, a local mermaid couple who stopped by once or twice a week, showed up not long after the exchange.

"Hey, guys," I said, thankful for the chance to wade out into the cool water. "Your usuals?"

"Yes, please," Amber replied. "Can you ask Bob to put it in a tall glass? I have to pick the kids up later, so I need to keep it between the water markers."

"Sure thing," I grinned. She was one of the sweetest people I'd ever known, and they were fat tippers to boot. I loved to see them pop up.

When I got back, Dax was giving Cass, who was knocking back shots with the gargoyles, the stink-eye. A couple months back, Cass had hit on one of Amber's sisters when she'd been in town for vacation. Of course, she'd gone full mermaid on him and had missed getting ahold of a wing tip by inches. That would have gone badly for Cass. Dax was still holding a grudge.

"The man's such a tool," he said. "Look at him. Taking shots like he's the one on vacation. And with gargoyles, no less. He has no shame."

"Just ignore him, sweetheart," Amber told him as I handed her a coconut rum and pineapple juice. "He's not worth it, right Des?"

9

"Right," I agreed as Dax took his draft beer from me. "Though I agree. I don't know what I did to piss off Karma. I thought I'd been a good girl."

Ignoring my attempt to be flip, Dax just shook his head, disdain coloring his features. "I don't get it. I mean, I know this is supposed to be his punishment for being the family embarrassment, but what did *we* do to deserve him?"

I'd asked myself that so many times I'd lost count. "I don't know, Dax. They probably didn't take us little people into consideration when the decision was made. They just got a kick out of forcing him into servitude."

"I guess," Dax said, then tore his gaze away and changed the subject. I chatted with them for a few minutes, enjoying the coolness of the water seeping into my crocks. The water bar extended out into the water several yards so that water creatures of all kinds could visit and was one of the resort's biggest moneymakers.

Sort of like a floating, covered dock, it was a long oval, with an elbow rest built all the way around it. Stools were attached sporadically as it extended farther offshore so land dwellers could enjoy their drinks in the water if they wanted. Most of the servers hated it because it required extra walking, but I loved it. It soothed my innate love of water and felt like heaven on my feet when the temperatures extended beyond hellfire.

A couple elves were making their way from the hotel to the tiki, so I left Amber and Dax to enjoy their drinks. One of the gargoyles snatched me by the wrist on my way past their table. I glared pointedly at his hand, then looked him in the eye.

"Three," I said.

"Three?" he queried, confused.

"Yeah, that's the number of seconds you have to let go of me if you wanna walk away with that hand still attached."

As I said it, I sent a little jolt of electricity skittering over the surface of my skin.

He jerked his hand back, glowering at me, but I didn't care; I was within my rights. According to resort policy, I had the right to defend myself and to refuse service to anybody who became physically or magically aggressive toward me.

"Now that we've all agreed to the basic playground rules of keeping our hands to ourselves, is there something I can get you, gentlemen?"

"Yeah," the one who hadn't grabbed me growled in a gravelly voice. "We want a round of strawberry daiquiris."

I furrowed my brow, wondering if he was being sarcastic. They weren't exactly daiquiri kinda guys. "Are you serious?"

"They said strawberry daiquiris, Maganti. Now!" Cass snapped, and my irritation bubbled. "Make mine mango, but bring five strawberries." He leered at his buddies. "We're expecting company, aren't we, fellas?"

"Well, then," I said, droll. "I'll hurry. I don't know the hourly rate of *company*, but I'd hate to waste your money."

"Speaking of hourly rates," Cassiel called as I spun on my heel and walked away, "how much were you making before you slept your way into one of the best positions on the island?"

I froze in place, rage tearing through me. Soft fur wound around my ankles.

Let it go, Destiny.

Tempest, my black and white fox familiar, nudged the back of my legs with her head.

You baited him, and you know he always has to one-up you. That was about ten up, but keep walking.

She was right, of course. I needed to learn to keep my mouth shut, but between our earlier exchange and the handsy incident, I wasn't feeling the love.

Fine. But I'm picturing him being crushed by a tsunami.

I'm okay with that as long as you don't actually conjure one. I hate getting wet. She shuddered.

I snorted. She never failed to make me feel better.

"You're a bigger woman than I am," Elsa, the elven woman, said when I stopped to greet them. "I would have turned him into a tree, then conjured pigeons."

Now there was a visual, along with a lesson. Don't mess with elves. They were beautiful to the point of being ethereal, but they were hard-core.

"He's a tool," I said, waving a dismissive hand in his direction. "You learn to live with him."

Tolthe, her husband, replied, "It took me three hundred years to reach your level of tolerance. You were not here the last time we were, but he heckled the poor brownie who'd taken your place to the point of tears. It's disturbing that he remains."

That was Cass, spreading sunshine everywhere he went. I suspected that played a huge part in why I was called back and why I had so much latitude. I don't think we'd had anybody stay there for more than a few weeks—other than me, of course.

"I wonder how Karma deals with angels," I said.

Elsa laughed. "I should hope the same as she does with all other beings. She is her own boss and a master bookkeeper."

"Then hope remains. It's nice to see you two, by the way." I smiled and took their orders, then headed to the bar.

I was surprised to see the hot werewolf was still sitting there. He hadn't spent much time at the bar beyond eating and sometimes working on his laptop. He glanced up and caught my eye, and I smiled. I was almost sure the corners of his mouth twitched into a brief smile before he glanced back down at his phone. That had happened a few times over the course of the week, and I couldn't help but wonder how he'd look smiling, his eyes glinting with humor.

He'd wear it well, I decided.

It took Bob a few minutes to make the drinks. While I was waiting, Stan tripped through behind me, spilling his drink down my leg and crashing into a table of fairies. Bamboo food containers flew from the table, and several drinks spilled.

"Dammit, Stan!" I snatched the glass out of his hand and swabbed the drinks off the table with the bar towel I kept tucked in my apron.

Fortunately, fairies are quick and they managed to escape before the liquid ran off and into their laps, but they didn't look pleased to have lost their lunches.

Stan's face reddened, and he began stuttering apologies. I waved him off when he tried to help. Bob came out from behind the bar to guide him back to his table, then returned to finish my drinks while I magicked the mess up. I'd worked in human restaurants before, and they'd sucked because I'd had to do everything by hand, sans magic. That had been such a time-suck.

It only took me a couple of minutes to have them squared away, including re-ordering the food, and Bob had fresh drinks on the bar a minute later.

Before I left to deliver the drinks, I glanced across the bar and was a little disappointed to see that werewolf guy was gone.

After dropping off drinks to Elsa and Tolthe, I made my way to Cass's table. Three ladies—the painted variety—had joined them. I set the drinks in front of them, biting my tongue to hold back the wide variety of snarky comments I was dying to make. Instead, I just took a deep breath, pictured the tsunami again, and asked if they were hungry.

The one with Cass licked her lips, then wrapped them around the straw in what I'm sure she thought was a sexy move. She missed the mark by about eight miles, at least in my opinion, but that was probably because I saw her glamour slip for just a second. I couldn't see what was under there, but if she considered what she was wearing an improvement, I'd hate to see her without the glamour.

I shuddered, surprised that as an angel, Cass fell for that trick. His beer goggles weren't doing him any favors.

Thankfully, not my circus, not my monkeys. I was the waitress, not the good-taste police.

A new couple had joined Amber and Dax out at the water bar, and I welcomed the chance to go out. My shoes were still a little sticky from the drink Stan spilled on me, and that would get miserable quickly.

I'd barely made it to the end of the dock when a high-pitched scream pierced the air behind me, nearly rupturing my eardrums. I handed Dax and Amber their drinks, and then, since the screaming hadn't abated, I raced back toward the beach. It crossed my mind that maybe one of Fiona's girls had come back and accidentally turned somebody to stone. I was always a little on edge when the gorgons were around. Great gals, but just thinking about their idea of fun gave me hives. And if that was what had happened, it was going to be a PR nightmare.

It only took me a few seconds to reach the end of the dock, and the screamer was still hard at it. I cringed, and several emotions flitted through my brain when I saw Cass slumped over the table, his fingers draped over his knocked-over daiquiri glass. Everything was still, until a tin of breath mints slipped out of his sagging shirt pocket and hit the concrete tiles.

The sticky, half-melted mango goo pooled under his face, and the eyes staring at me were sightless. I'd never seen his face relaxed and peaceful, and I realized for the first time how beautiful a man he must have been at some point.

A ray of golden light began to stream from the center of his back, pulling upward into a string until, as the last of it trailed from his body, it shot straight toward the sky, disappearing into the rays of the sun.

"Well," said a bored voice behind me, and I turned to see Steph, a Valkyrie, leaning on the bar with one elbow, rockin' the daylights out of a black and gold bikini. "It looks like this place is about to get a lot more pleasant. Which one of you finally manned—or womanned—up and did it?"

I looked around, wondering the same thing, and was surprised to see that everybody else was looking at me.

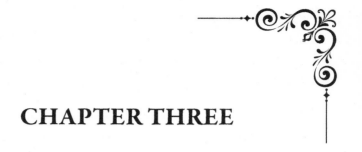

CHAPTER THREE

"OH, NO," I SAID, SHAKING my head. "I've wished for it a thousand times, but I didn't do it."

"Nobody would cast blame if you did, lass," Tolthe said gently. Faerie law was much different than witch law, the rules I had to abide by. By their law, I could have called Cass out a hundred times over and been within my rights, but witches had, by necessity, modernized. Also, I was pretty sure there was a policy somewhere in my employee handbook that made it against the rules to kill your boss.

I held up my hands. "First things first. How do we know he didn't just ... I don't know ... choke to death or have a heart attack?"

One of the women who had been with them glared at me. Probably because she and her gal-pals weren't going to get paid now that he was dead. "He didn't choke or have a heart attack. We were sitting right there. He just dropped dead midsentence." She preened. "Right when he was tellin' me how sexy he thought I was."

Another of the gum-snappers, this one wearing a shimmering blue beach wrap that was three sizes too small, shook her head, her huge hair barely moving. "Nope. Wasn't no heart attack I've ever seen, and I've seen plenty."

Heaving a huge sigh, I glanced down at Tempest.

Will you go tell Blake we need him?

She gave a curt nod and disappeared into thin air. A year ago, I would have told him myself, since we'd been engaged. But I sort of lost the desire to deal with him at all when he confessed he'd kissed his secretary. I'm odd like that.

Still, he was the executive director of the resort—the reason Cass had made the crack about sleeping my way to the top.

I picked my way around the table because nobody else was moving and placed my finger on his carotid. Nothin'. Nada. Zip.

"Oh, he's dead, Des," Amber said, crossing her arms and biting her lip. She and Dax, along with their friends, had assumed human form and followed me up the dock. "We all saw his essence leave. There's no putting that genie ... err, angel ... back in the bottle."

"Then everybody needs to stay put," I said, trying to get a handle on the situation. "Blake's gonna want to talk to everybody here. Did anybody see anything?"

A popping noise behind me was followed by a deep voice that still gave me chills as well as pissed me off. "Excellent question, but our security team will take it from here. I'm sure they'll want to talk to everybody individually rather than as a group."

His sharp blue eyes turned to me. "Destiny, I believe you'd be a good place to start. I'll meet you in the office in five minutes."

"I need to clean this up," I protested, a little bit in shock. The waitress in me had apparently taken over because all I could see was the mess. The whole situation was beginning to feel surreal. He'd complained about a couple cups on the ground earlier, yet there he was, sprawled on his table in a puddle of orange.

"That's not really the priority," Blake said, a ghost of a smile on his lips. I wanted to punch him because there was also a huge dose of concern on his face, and the last thing I wanted was that.

You need to get your poop in a group, Destiny. Tempest butted her head against my leg.

I glanced down at her deceptively innocent face into her translucent green eyes and struggled to pull myself together. It wasn't like me to fall apart in a crisis. I sucked in a deep breath through my nose, then blew it out through my mouth, centering myself.

"Okay," I said to Blake. "I'll be in Cass's office."

"Wait," he said, realizing at the same time I did how compromising that could be. "Just take a seat at the bar until I can get to you."

Security personnel rushed past me to the body on my way to the bar. I scooted up onto one bar stool, and Tempest jumped onto another. Bob pushed a glass of lime water toward me, and I took a gulp, my mouth as dry as sand.

"What do you think happened?" I asked, more to fill the silence than anything else.

"From what I can see, somebody up and killed him," he said, raising a furry shoulder as he wiped the bar.

"No shit, Sherlock," I said, rolling my eyes. "But how, do you think? It almost had to be poison."

"Yeah," he said, drawing his bushy eyebrows down, "but what type of poison kills an angel?"

"I didn't know you could kill an angel, period," Tempest said. She didn't usually speak in public, but it was more because she was a bit of a snob than because she couldn't. The attention made her nuts. Bob was an exception though, and I suspect it had as much to do with the food he snuck her as it did with the fact he was just a nice guy all around.

I turned the question over and over in my mind. I wasn't an earth witch, so I had no idea what blend of herbs would be lethal to an angel. I had some friends and family who were hearth witches, but I sucked at herbology. I mean, I knew deities were pretty much immortal unless you had their Kryptonite, so to speak. But angels may be another story altogether.

"Oh, that's easy," Elsa said as she and Tolthe joined us at the bar. Elsa was right in her element; as an elf, nature was her thing.

"Not for all of us," I said, smiling down into her crystal-blue eyes. "Care to enlighten the rest of the class?"

"None," she said, shrugging.

"What do you mean, none?" I asked.

Tolthe smiled. "No poison—at least none in the traditional sense—could kill an angel. They're immune to everything in nature. The only lethal concoction he could have ingested would have been a death elixir."

She had me stumped. "Okay. That sounds suspiciously close to a poison."

"No," she said, shaking her head. "Well, yes, but it has much more than just herbs in it. It has to be brewed using death essence."

Elves were exhausting. They were quite literal and, because they were also brilliant, tended to assume everybody else knew exactly what they were talking about. This time, though, I had an inkling.

"You mean it can't be made by just anybody. Or, more accurately, it can't be made using anything the average person has access to."

"Exactly," Tolthe replied.

"All right," Tempest growled, scowling. "Plain English."

Surprisingly, it was Bob who answered. "It had to come from an angel of death. You know, a reaper."

Despite what most humans believed, there wasn't just one reaper. It was one of the sillier beliefs, in my opinion. I mean, thousands of people died every second. Let's be realistic. Even assuming one being could manage such a colossal task, the overtime pay alone would be off the chain. And what if the poor guy caught the flu or something?

"Come again?" I said. "You're saying a reaper did this?" As far as I knew, reaper magic was genetic, just like my magic. They touched somebody with the intent of separating the soul from the body, and *poof*—the person was a goner, but I was almost positive they couldn't transfer their magic or have it stolen.

"Not necessarily," Elsa said. "Reaper magic leaves a residue in the body for a minute or two just to make sure it takes, so to speak. Death essence can be harvested from the body after the angel leaves, but it's complicated. I can only think of a handful of people, elves included, who could do it."

"Okay then, so we're dealing with either a reaper or somebody with some powerful juju," I said.

"Yeah." Bob nodded his head, causing a clump of hair-gelled fur to fall forward over his forehead. "Or somebody who bought it off the black market."

I threw my hands in the air. "Oh for crying out loud! You just told me it was rare and special, and now you tell me you can buy it at the same place you buy knock-off Rolexes and TVs that fell off the truck?"

Bob made the iffy gesture with his hand. "Not quite that simple because you need a ton of money and the right connections, but you have the right idea. Reapers are supposed to stay around long enough for the essence to evaporate, but they have huge caseloads."

"Could a reaper have been the one responsible?" I asked.

Tolthe pressed his lips together. "It's possible, but I can't imagine it. Reapers are rigorously vetted, and the penalty for killing even an excommunicated angel is ... far worse than death. They'd be insane to risk it."

Elsa cleared her throat loud enough to catch my attention and tipped her head toward the whole hot mess behind me. "Your former beloved is on his way, along with his head of security."

I scowled. "Please don't use that term. I prefer *the loathsome lip-locker*, or you can just say *asshat ex*."

She laughed, the sound tinkling. "Well, whatever your preference, Blake is on his way over here, and he doesn't look pleased."

CHAPTER FOUR

I TOOK A DEEP BREATH and turned in the direction she was looking. Sure enough, Tall, Dark, and Despicable was stomping toward me with a muscle-bound meathead, and both of them looked like they'd just sucked a lemon.

I crossed my arms, put on my best bored expression, and waited for them to come to me.

This is not the time to cop an attitude, Tempest reminded me. *You and Cass weren't exactly BFFs, and now somebody's pulled his plug.*

Yeah, yeah, I replied, knowing she was right. It was impossible for me to smile at him, though, so "bored" was the best expression I could manage.

"Destiny," Blake said, inclining his head toward me. Muscles didn't bother to say anything.

"Blake," I replied, trying to read his expression. Normally, he could control everything except his eyes; they were always a combination of regret and sadness when he looked at me. Today though, they were inscrutable.

"If you'll follow me, I have some questions."

He led me back to the office, and the guard followed, sandwiching me in between the two of them so I couldn't run even if I wanted to. Tempest kept tight to my ankles, trotting along beside me.

There was barely room for all of us in the cramped, cluttered office space, so Blake moved around behind the desk and motioned to a chair across from him. Cass, being the overbearing jerk that he was, always had the seat adjusted so that it was lower than his was; a mental mind-screw meant to intimidate. I chose to stand, placing my hands on the back of my chair instead.

"Cass is dead," he said, stating the obvious.

"Yeah, I gathered as much from the lack of bitterness on his face and the mango slush dripping unheeded off his nose."

Blake slammed his fist on the desk, causing a container of breath mints to bounce. My mind disconnected for a second and focused on the metallic clang rather than the anger and frustration oozing from Blake's every pore.

Tempest shot me a glare.

I sighed. "Look, I don't know what you want me to say. I was out on the water bar talking to Amber and Dax. I heard a scream and came running back to shore, and that's when I saw him. A couple seconds later, his essence left, and that was it. I asked Tempest to get you."

He rubbed his temples. "See, the thing is, a couple of patrons heard you wish him dead not fifteen minutes before he keeled over."

I snorted. "If me wishing him dead actually caused it, he'da been a goner the first day we met. You know as well as I do he's hated me from day one."

"I realize that and also know why, but that's beside the point. What matters is that the feeling was mutual, and—"

He turned to the guard. "Step outside for a minute, please."

For a second, the guy hesitated but then turned and did as he was told.

Blake leaned his elbows on the desk, moving closer to me. He lowered his voice. "You have ... access to death essence."

"Me?" My voice was about three octaves higher than normal. Blake glanced toward the door, and I lowered my voice. "How do you figure *I* have access to it? I didn't even know it was a thing until five minutes ago when Elsa explained it to me."

He drew his brows down. "You and I both know how you have access."

I ran my tongue over my teeth and struggled to maintain my cool. He was talking about my brother, Michael. In his misspent youth, he'd wasted quite a bit of his time in unsavory places. When his best friend was killed in an alley, it scared him straight and he became an agent with the Paranormal Criminal Investigations Bureau.

The contacts he'd made during his years on the dark side proved useful in his career, and he'd quickly climbed the ladder.

I narrowed my eyes at the implication. "You know as well as I do, Mike went straight years ago when he joined the PCIB."

He dipped his head and pulled in a breath. "You know that and I know that, but it's bound to come out. That gives you motive, opportunity, and ability."

I plopped down in the chair but reached beneath it to raise it up so I was eye-level with Blake. "You know I didn't do this."

After searching my face for a few seconds, he said, "I know you didn't. But I also know it's only a matter of time before they find out about Michael, and then you're done. They'll bury you."

The worst part of it was that he wasn't necessarily being figurative. In many situations, this one included, the penalty for murder was death if the location fell under PCIB jurisdiction, which the Enchanted Coast did. With such a wide variety of species that could kill with just a look or touch, they had to take a hard stance on it.

"So what are you saying?" I asked.

The familiar pleading look was back in his eyes.

"I'm saying that I'm going to do everything I can to clear you from this side, but you're going to have to dig in, too. I don't have the same access you do to people. Find out who saw what." He ran his fingers through his hair. "In essence, dig like your life depends on it, because it does."

Well, then. I had to hand it to him; he really knew how to motivate a girl.

CHAPTER FIVE

HE CALLED HIS MUSCLENESS back in and proceeded to grill me on who I'd seen Cass talk to, what he'd said to me, where I'd seen him go, and who'd been in the bar and on the beach while he was there.

"Does anybody in particular stand out to you?"

I thought, but nothing was outside the norm. Of course, that covered a lot of ground when the clientele ranged from drunken cupids to vampire young. I shrugged helplessly. "No. We had our regulars, then we had several tables of vacationers."

"Did Jim stop by?"

Jim was a reaper who usually stopped in a couple times a week when he had a day off. He was one of those quiet guys who just wanted to have a couple beers and relax. He usually hung out with Stan or Evan, probably because both of them were immune to his magic. If he had a little too much to drink, he didn't have to worry about killing them if they helped him up.

"No," I replied. "As a matter of fact, he hasn't been in all week that I know of."

He thought for a couple of minutes, and the silence became uncomfortable.

I glanced toward the door. "Are we finished?"

"For now," he said. "And Tempest?"

My little fox turned to him, brow raised.

"Thank you for coming to get me. I'm glad you're at Destiny's side."

She tilted her head at him, and something passed between them, though it was brief.

As soon as the door clicked shut, I asked her about it out loud.

"He simply asked me to stay by your side and take care of you."

"Why would he say that?"

"He still cares about you, Destiny."

"Then he probably should have kept his lips to himself," I said, irritated by just the thought.

"I'm not saying he gets a pass, just that he knows he screwed up and that it's not a good idea to ostracize him right now. Now that handsome werewolf..."

I smiled. "He is kinda hot, isn't he?"

"Pfft. He's a predator. That's part of his arsenal."

"I don't know," I said. "I think that's more a vampire thing. Werewolves don't need to attract food. And besides, it's gauche to eat people these days."

She laughed. "Yeah, I'm sure that's why it's passed out of fad."

"Well?" Bob said once I made it back to the bar. "What did he say?"

"Nothing. Just asked me about our argument this morning and about who was here."

He set several drinks onto the server's deck. "These are for table five. Did he mention any suspects?"

"Yeah," I said, barking out a dry laugh. "Me."

I scooped up the tray and went to greet the group. When I made my way out to the beach tables, I noticed they'd taken Cass away but hadn't cleaned up the mess. Great, the man was a pain in my backside to the very end.

The last thing I wanted to deal with was mango slime that had dripped off a dead angel, or anything dead, for that matter, but it didn't look like I had a choice.

Amber and Dax had left, probably to get the kids, but Elsa and Tolthe were there for the week. After I cleaned up the mess, I took them another round of drinks, then cringed when Blake's voice raked across my nerves yet again.

"Des, I need you to watch the bar while I talk to Bob," he said.

I gave him a thumbs-up, unwilling to walk back and interact with him face-to-face again.

"You know, it's likely you'll be seeing much more of him, at least until this is resolved," Elsa said, a dry smile curving her plump lips.

"Yeah, I know," I said with a huff, "but that doesn't mean I have to like it."

I stopped by a couple tables on my way back to the bar and cast a glance down to the deck of the water bar just to make sure nobody was waiting for me there. Even though there was a service bell, I'd found many people thought it was rude to actually ring it to get my attention.

I stepped behind the bar to make my drink and shifted the fan in my direction. Ah, one of the first benefits of Cass being dead, I thought as the cool air brushed over my sticky skin. I felt like that thought should have made me feel bad, but it really didn't. He'd been a horrible person. I wasn't exactly glad he was dead, but I was grateful I'd never have to deal with him again.

While I was waiting for a Guinness to pour, I wondered who his replacement would be. Probably Bob, at least for the interim.

Within fifteen minutes or so, the place was filled to capacity. Nothing like a good murder to bring in the crowds. The chatter bounced back and forth between tables, each sharing the information they'd already picked up.

I grinned as I hustled my buns off to serve everybody; being from a small town, I was intimately familiar with the efficiency of the gossip tree, and the resort was its own little community. The only difference between the human world and the paranormal one was that there wasn't such an underlying need to be fake about it or pretend to be sorry when you weren't.

The place took on an almost festive air, and I smiled to myself as I thought about making a drink special in honor of the occasion. Maybe use a little Midori or KeKe liqueur to give it a green tint. Call it the Cass is Grass Martini.

Probably too soon, and definitely indelicate, but again, I was dealing with people who drank blood, ate raw fish, and shot people in the ass with heart arrows for a living. Political correctness really wasn't a thing. Me being a suspect was, though, so I figured it would be best to at least pretend to maintain a modicum of propriety.

Bob filed back out of office, jumping behind the bar when he saw how busy we'd gotten.

"Wow," he said. "Gossipmongers, or is everybody just as happy as we are?"

I smacked him on the arm as I filled my tray with the drinks I'd just made. I just needed the beer and wine. "I'm not really glad he's dead. Can you pour me three house reds and grab me a couple bottles of Big Wave?"

He cocked a brow at me. "Yeah, you sound real tore up about it."

"Pfft. It's no skin off my nose, but I'm not glad about it. Pretending I was torn up would be suspicious for sure. I'm just ... ambivalent and choosing to see the silver lining."

I pushed back through the crowd, and eventually somebody stuffed a few bucks in the jukebox. It was hard *not* to feel at least a little bit of the positive energy of the crowd when everybody was laughing and Buffett floated on the tropical breeze.

CHAPTER SIX

"WOW, WHAT A NIGHT," I told Bob once the last customer had cleared out. I was thankful the tiki was only open until eleven. It was almost midnight, and the party hadn't stopped since that afternoon.

We hadn't been that busy since the last leprechaun wedding we'd hosted. Now *those* folks could drink. They were tight with their gold though, so it was always a good idea to add the gratuity to their check rather than depend on their generosity.

Vampires and weres on the other hand? Fat tippers in general, but the job was a little more hazardous because they tended to play rough.

I took off a shoe and flexed my foot, pulling my toes back toward my shins and rolling my ankles.

Bob collapsed on a chair beside me. "You ain't kiddin'," he said.

"Grab the drawer," I said. "You count, and I'll clean."

With a few flicks of my wrist, the mop was chasing the broom across the worn wooden planks of the floor, and the beer was floating from the stockroom, filling the coolers.

He shook his head. "I loved Glendelle"—the brownie he worked with before me—"but I gotta say, you're much more handy at closing time."

It didn't take him any time at all to count the till, separating out the credit card receipts from the room charges. I ran the cash-out slip from my register and did the same thing. When I was done, I had a nice stack of cash left over.

"Not too shabby," I said as I finished counting my tips. "Did you do okay?"

He was grinning. "A little better than okay, I'd say."

We both made more than we usually made in three nights, and considering we had dirt cheap room and board at the resort, it was basically pure profit.

"I do feel a little bad, though," he said. "I mean, we made most of it because Cass was murdered."

I lifted a shoulder. "Don't look at it like that. He'd be dead regardless of whether we made ten dollars or ten thousand."

He lumbered back behind the bar and poured two shots of Irish whiskey and handed me one.

"To Cass," he said.

"May he finally have that stick out of his ass," I said, clinking glasses. In truth, I really did hope he was happy. I'd always suspected he was miserable for a reason, and nobody knew the true story behind why he got the boot.

I grimaced as I took the shot, and Tempest spoke aloud. "You know, you should be careful saying things like that. I know what you meant, but others may not."

The mop and broom were finished and hovering outside the closet, so I opened the door with the swish of a couple fingers and put them away.

"Like who? There's nobody else around."

"Like me," Blake said, stepping off the dark path from the hotel and into the light.

I sighed. "You know I didn't do it just as well as Bob does. Now if you had one of your minions with you, that would be another story."

He scowled at the term. "You know those are some of the most highly trained magical investigators and guards on the planet, right?"

"They still look like goons," I said, slipping my feet back into my shoes.

"Any progress?" Bob asked.

Blake shook his head. "Not yet, but I forgot to leave the keys earlier." He pulled some keys out of his pocket and handed them to me.

"What am I supposed to do with them?" I asked, confused.

"Do you mind being interim manager until I can find somebody?"

Color me shocked. That was the last thing I expected to hear, but then again, I expected whatever he had to say to be punctuated by one of his gorillas putting cuffs on me.

"I don't mind, but do you think it's a good idea, considering I'm suspect numero uno?"

"Since I'm executive director of the resort, I get to decide what's a good idea, so yes. I think it's a good idea. You've done the job before and done it well. I'd offer it to you full time once this is all over if I thought you'd take it."

He slid onto a stool beside me, and I was irritated because the smell of his cologne still made my heart stutter.

Scowling, I moved down a stool under the pretense of reaching for Bob's drawer so I could do the second count and deposit it into the magical safe in Cass's office—well, I guess now it was my office. From there, it went directly to the accounting department.

As always, his count was right. Blake walked around the bar and pulled out three beers, handing one to me and one to Bob, and keeping one for himself.

"We have to figure this out," he said, raking his fingers through his hair. "For cripe's sake, an *angel* was murdered at my resort. And to make matters worse, you're the one everybody's gonna be looking at. Assigning you interim manager is a proactive step to show my confidence in you, but we need to solve this thing," he said.

Bob cracked his beer and took a big swig. "We're not exactly detectives," he said. "It's not like we're golfing with these people."

"No," Blake said, waving his bottle toward Bob, "You're nonthreatening and, if memory serves, a damned good bartender. People talk to you."

"That's true," I said. "It never ceases to amaze me that you're seven feet tall and have hands that could crush skulls but still manage to come across as harmless. People are more scared of *me* than they are of you."

"That's because you're terrifying," Bob said.

"What? I am not. I'm one of the friendliest people I know. And I'm like a foot and half shorter and a buck-fifty lighter than you." I raised a brow at Blake, telling him to back me up. It was the least he could do, really.

He pinched his lips together and pointed at me. "That look right there," he said. "That's terrifying. I'm afraid to disagree with you, and I'm a ninth-level wizard. Don't get me wrong. You're friendly, too. People love you. But you're a prime example that they're not mutually exclusive traits."

"Why do you think Cass had it out for you so bad?" Bob asked.

Blake's words from earlier drifted back to me. He said he'd known why Cass didn't like me.

"You two should probably fill me in on that because I've been working with the jerk for two years now and haven't been able to figure it out."

They both looked at me like I was nuts. Or blind. I couldn't figure out which.

"You didn't know?" Bob asked, scratching his head.

"Know what?" I felt like I was the only one who was missing the punchline of a joke.

"There was a reason he got the manager's job when you declined it. He got it because the higher-ups wanted him to emulate you."

"Come again," I said, raising my brows. Surely I hadn't heard that right.

"You're exactly what he was supposed to be but wasn't," Blake said. "People love you but don't walk on you. You have a temper, but you control it. You love cake and beer as much as the next person, but you eat and drink in moderation. You know how to walk the fine line between enough and too much—at least most of the time—but he couldn't, or wouldn't, figure it out. It's what made him so horrible at his job—this one and the angel gig. He always went too far one way or the other. Temperance, remember?"

I snorted. "I'm the poster child for a lot of things, but temperance isn't one of them."

"Okay," Bob said, then pulled another beer for each of us from the cooler.

I eyeballed the beer because it had been a hell of a day but sighed and waved him off. "I'm good. I have to be here to open in the morning, and heat and hangovers don't mix."

Blake raised a brow at me. "Oh, the irony."

Glowering at him, I snatched the beer from him just to prove him wrong.

CHAPTER SEVEN

EIGHT HOURS LATER, I really regretted that second beer. I was a lightweight when it came to drinking, and between the shot and the two beers, I'd gone to bed with a bit of a buzz. Thankfully, Elena, a cute Italian vampire, was waitressing that day, so all I'd have to do was schmooze and help out as needed. Unlike Cass, I just didn't have it in me to let the place go down in flames rather than jump in and help.

She was good at her job and wasn't afraid to work, so the most I ended up doing all day was bussing a few tables and refilling a few drinks. Besides that, I took advantage of the time to talk to folks who'd been there the day before.

Though I worked it into conversation, I managed to find out in one way or another exactly what everybody was doing there. Considering there were only a few people missing from the day before, it wasn't hard. By the end of the day, the only people I couldn't nail down were the mystery werewolf, a gorgon who wasn't there with Fiona's group, and a couple witches who'd managed to fly under my radar.

Bob was working again, and I jumped in and helped him when the gorgon group came for lunch at the same time a bunch of nymphs showed up at the water bar. We worked through the tickets, and once we were through the rush, I helped him clean up.

"So, no mysterious werewolf guy today?" I asked, restocking the cooler with Cabern-A, one of the blood wines we used in our vampire sangrias and wine slushies. I wasn't much for the cutesy name, but the vampire portion of our undead community loved it.

He shot me a sideways glance as he set down an extra case of Miller Lite he'd just brought up from the back. "I wouldn't go so far as to call him mysterious," he said. "He just wasn't much of a talker. It's not like he was using John Doe on his credit card."

He put his hand to his chin and wrinkled his forehead. "Though I did actually *know* a John Doe once. British cyclops. The man kicked ass at darts but couldn't play poker for squat."

I tilted my head and took a deep breath, waiting for him to catch back up.

"Sorry," he said. "I think of that guy every time I hear the name."

"That's only logical, since it *was* his name," I said. "But what I need to know is the werewolf's name. And did he say what he was doing here?"

"His name was Colin Moore, and he said he was here on business."

"What business?" I asked, frustrated. "It's your job to dig this information out of people."

"No," he said, drawing the word out. "It's my job to provide an excellent customer experience. And for him, that was keeping his beer full and making sure his steak was cooked right."

He was right. I'd seen him trying to engage the dude and falling flat.

"But I did happen to overhear some of his conversation with Cass while I was uh ... cleaning the cooler," he said, looking smug. "For some reason, people forget Sasquatches have excellent hearing."

I grinned. The coolers were self-cleaning, but Cass wouldn't have known that because he never sullied himself behind the bar. Leaning a little closer because he wasn't the only paranormal with super-hearing, I said, "I knew it was bugging you, too! What did you hear?"

"That part's kinda disappointing," he said. "It didn't make much sense to me, but Cass wasn't happy about it. They reviewed some paperwork, and Cass stormed off when the guy mentioned something about a decision. Mr. Moore didn't show much reaction. He just kinda watched him, speculating. I got the feeling he didn't like him much, though."

That caught my attention. "What gave you that feeling?"

Bob lifted a shoulder. "Just the way he looked at him, kinda like Cass was centaur crap on the bottom of his shoe. After that, every other time Cass came out of his office and saw the werewolf, he looked pissed and avoided him. Then yesterday, while you were down at the water, Cass came to the bar to get more whipped cream—"

I cut him off with a snortle, and he held up his hand.

"I know," he said, closing his eyes, "but please—I'm giving it my best shot *not* to get that visual. Anyway, when he came to the bar, Moore told him they needed to talk, but Cass ignored him. Moore called after him that Cass was forcing him to do something he didn't want to do, and then he left."

He finished polishing the wineglass in his hand.

"So, that didn't strike you as worth mentioning before now, maybe?" I asked.

"It did, but Blake said somebody else had already mentioned it to him. Besides, the dude was long gone by the time Cass bit it."

Tempest sighed from her spot at the end of the bar.

For somebody lookin' at hard time or death, you're not puttin' much effort into this.

I thought back to the incident with Stan the day before, when he'd spilled his drink on me and knocked all the food off the table. Bob had been in the process of making the daiquiris for Cass's table.

When I reminded him of that, a look of dawning crossed his face. "I'd forgotten all about that. Those drinks weren't three feet from him—it would have been cake for him to reach across and add something to it. For that matter, a few people could have done it."

"It looks like we finally have at least one suspect who isn't me, then," I said, picking up my phone. It was time to do a little checking up on Colin Moore.

CHAPTER EIGHT

THE FIRST PERSON I called was Blake, since he'd told Bob somebody else had talked to him about Colin. Rather than the cooperation I'd expected after our talk in the office, he stonewalled me.

"It wasn't Colin, Destiny," he said. "You're just going to have to trust me."

"Trust you?" I bit out before I could stop myself.

I could practically see his spine stiffen, and it reflected in the tone of his voice. "Yes, trust me. Mr. Moore isn't the one who killed Cass."

"And how, exactly, do you know that? He had at least one conversation with Cass, and it didn't go well. After that, Cass avoided him like the plague, and the guy told him he was forcing him to do something he didn't want to do."

"Yeah, I know all that already," he said. "Unless you saw him drop the essence in with your own two eyes, drop him off the list, though."

"List?" I snapped, "He *is* the list. Oh, and don't forget about me."

He heaved a deep breath. "I wish I could tell you more—really, I do—but my hands, and my lips, are tied on this. You have to take me at my word." He lowered his voice. "You may think I'm a lot of things, Des, but you have to admit I've never lied to you."

I had to admit that was the truth, even though I would have rather pulled one of my own teeth than say it out loud. He wasn't a liar.

"That doesn't necessarily mean you're right, though," I said. "Maybe it just means you're telling me what you've been told."

"No, I've been thoroughly briefed on his mission here. I'm not being told anything about that one way or another, but knowing why he was here, I can tell you he didn't kill him. Plus, I played a couple rounds of golf with him, and I didn't get any bad vibes."

One of Blake's superpowers was sensing the truth. He was a literal walking, talking lie detector. Just like most powers, though, it wasn't infallible.

I knew that for a fact because there'd been a few times I'd had to work around it during our relationship in order to plan surprises or avoid him guessing what he got for Christmas. I was a stickler for that because presents should always be a surprise—that was half the fun.

"Did you discuss the murder with him? Ask him flat-out if he did it?"

"No," he said, biting out the word. "I haven't seen him since it happened."

"Well then, we can't rule him out."

"Destiny—"

"No, Blake." I was beyond the point of irritation. "He had opportunity and maybe ability. At least as much as I have, anyway. He wasn't getting along with Cass for whatever reason, and I'm sorry, but he yelled a threat across a bar not fifteen minutes before Cass bit it. So, why should I be on the suspect list but he shouldn't?"

"You're not gonna let this go, are you?"

"Not unless you give me a reason to. Putting off positive vibes during golf doesn't quite meet that standard."

We'd come to an impasse. As far as I was concerned, Colin Moore was at least as good for the murder as I was, and I only knew for a fact that one of us was innocent.

After I hung up with Blake, I helped Elena and Bob get ready for the dinner rush.

Celeste, a succubus, was leaning against the bar doing a much better job of making a straw look sexy than Cass's date had done. I sighed.

"Hey, Destiny," she said.

"Hey, Celeste," I answered, giving her a small half smile. One of the safety enchantments of the resort dampened the allure of predatory creatures such as succubi, incubi, and sirens, but that didn't do anything about her natural assets—legs that went on forever, glistening hair that curled halfway down her back even in its ponytail, or the almond-shaped eyes that screamed sex.

To her credit, she came to the resort exactly because of the enchantment, and I got it. She was three hundred years old and looked thirty. A *hot* thirty. She was perfectly suited to her career as a litigation attorney, but her powers of persuasion were a personal hindrance.

I couldn't imagine not even being able to run to the grocery store in sweats and an old T-shirt without turning on the bag boy when I accidentally made eye contact to say thank you.

Still, she could wear a potato sack and look better than most of us even without the enchantments. I'd hate her a little, but she was too much of a sweetheart.

"Did you work things out with Blake yet?" she asked.

I scowled at her. "No! Why would you even think that?"

She lifted a shoulder. "I don't know. I just figured he'd have worn you down by now."

"No," I said, my stomach turning. "There's no wearing me down. I can't come back from that."

"Okay, sweetie." She pushed herself onto the stool behind her and crossed one leg over the other. "What else is new, then?"

"How much time you got?" I asked with a dry smile.

She patted the stool beside her. "I'm here for a week. That enough time?"

"It's a start." I slid onto the stool and told her about the whole Cass debacle.

"Well," she said, "I can't say I'm sorry he's dead, but I will say I'm surprised. I didn't know angels could die, except at the hands of other angels."

"You know," I said, rubbing my chin, "that's a good point. I didn't either, until Elsa told me about it. Is it common knowledge and I was just the last to know?"

"I didn't know either," Bob said, "and I've been around awhile."

"I doubt they want it advertised," she said, adjusting her bathing suit top when she noticed a surfer-boy vampire staring at her cleavage. She narrowed her eyes at him, and he snapped his gaze to the bar in front of him. On the supernatural food chain, tricentenarian sex demon ranked way higher than postpubescent undead.

"I'm trying to think of where I've heard the werewolf's name before," she went on, fishing a cherry out of the bottom of the drink with her straw. "It's familiar, but I can't think of why."

"So should I take Blake's word for it and drop it?"

She cocked an eyebrow at me. "Honey, I literally mess with men's minds to survive, both financially and physically. If there's one thing I know, it's that nobody's mind is impervious to suggestion. It's your hide on the line, and somebody killed an angel. That's no joke. I wouldn't take anybody's word for anything."

Truer words.

I hopped off the stool and headed back to my office, grabbing a lime water on my way. "Then I have some uncomfortable calls to make."

CHAPTER NINE

AS BAD AS I HATED TO, I was gonna have to call my brother. Blake was right about one thing—Michael knew the dark underbelly of the paranormal world. The problem would be getting ahold of him.

I was pulling his number up on my phone when Tempest blinked into my office, causing my ears to pop. She landed in the chair across from me.

"Where have you been?"

She took the time to lick her paw before she answered. "I was up snooping around in Blake's office. I heard what he told you, and I don't like that he's apparently under some kind of magical gag order. Those come with too many strings."

I waited for her to continue, but she went back to licking her paws.

"So," I said, impatient. "Did you find anything?"

"Oh, yeah." She looked up at me, her fuzzy little brow furrowed. "Actually, it's what I *didn't* find that's interesting."

"And what was that?" Talking to a fox was similar to talking to a cat; they thought in different patterns than we did, so some patience was required. She was smart and analytical though, so it was rarely time wasted.

"An address for Colin Moore, or any personal information for that matter. I found credit-card receipts, a phone number, and menu preferences. That's it."

"That was all that was on his guest sheet?"

"Yep," she said, popping the p. "Weird, right?"

"I'll say." The guest-registry sheet for the resort was necessarily long. When you dealt with such a wide array of species, even the drilled-down list was extensive. I'd been itching to get my fingers on it and streamline it since I started, but it hadn't made my priorities while I was dating Blake, then when it all blew up, helping him run the place was akin to going to the dentist, the gyno, and the DMV all at the same time.

I'd met him a few months after I started working there when he'd brought a group of shifter investors to lunch at the tiki. I'd never seen him in all that time, then all of a sudden, I was seeing him everywhere. He'd stop in for a drink after work, or I'd run into him at the employee pool.

We talked, and it took me more than a month to figure out he wanted to ask me out but was afraid to because of his position. So, I asked him. The hotel didn't have a dating policy per se—we had enough rules and regulations as it was.

To cover the little stuff like injuries and sexual harassment, we signed arbitration clauses when we were hired, and trust me—frivolous lawsuits weren't an issue. The arbitration committee was made up of harpies, and you *did not* want to go before them either as a plaintiff or defendant unless you absolutely had to. It kept everybody straight on both sides of the aisle.

Anyway, we followed the standard lovey-dovey song and dance. Despite what Cass had said, I hadn't slept my way into any position. I'd been doing the same job since the day I started. The only thing that had changed was as I gained seniority, I got better shifts and more responsibility—standard practice in most jobs.

He proposed on our second anniversary, under a full moon on the beach. Then less than a month later, he told me he'd kissed his secretary but tried to explain it away. I hadn't even known there was an attraction.

So, that was the story of Blake and Destiny, no less, no more.

It's only relevant because in the time I'd known him, I'd learned that he was a stickler for paperwork. Every box must be checked, every line filled out. So the fact that Mr. Moore's paperwork was so lacking was puzzling, indeed.

"I was just about to call Michael," I told Tempest.

"I think that's a grand idea," she said. "And ask him how hard it is to actually get ahold of the death essence." She tilted her head to the side. "On second thought, don't ask him anything over the phone. Let's meet him for lunch instead."

"Are you suggesting that because you're worried somebody's listening or because you want to see Rocky again?" Rocky was my brother's wolf familiar, and Tempest had a soft spot for him.

She made a show of examining her paw, even though she'd just cleaned it.

"You never know who's listening," she said, trying to be sage. "After all, an angel was killed. This is gonna be top priority for every law-enforcement agency on the planet."

"That's it?" I asked.

"Well, and it'll be nice to see them, too. Rocky has such soft-looking fur, but that air of danger ..." She gave a little shudder and grinned.

"Wicked fox," I said, smiling back. "But I agree. It'll be good to see Michael. And Rocky. It's been too long."

I hit *call* and was disappointed but not surprised when it went to voicemail. If he were on an undercover job somewhere, he wouldn't be able to answer.

He was good about calling me back, though, so I decided to move on and just go up to the resort and talk to Blake face-to-face. He wasn't the only one with a bullshit meter, and I wanted to see where he pinged on mine.

CHAPTER TEN

EVEN THOUGH I WAS ONE of the few employees with porting privileges, I opted to walk. I loved running my fingers across the top of the sea oats, and the packed sugar sand felt good beneath my feet. It also gave me time to think about how I was going to approach Blake again, considering he'd been so firm on the phone.

The more I thought about it, the more hopeless it felt. There had been at least five people who had access to the drinks on the table. I didn't consider them to be particularly viable though, considering four of them plus Cass would have had to be distracted enough for one of them to slip the essence into his daiquiri unseen.

Out of that group, the gargoyles were the most suspicious, if only because the girls didn't strike me as the sharpest crayons in the box. Besides, with Cass dead, I doubt they got paid. The gargoyles, on the other hand, were shady. I doubted there was any honor among that particular group of thieves, and gargoyles were known for being ruthless.

If Cass had crossed one of them—or all of them for that matter—they wouldn't have hesitated to off him if they stood to profit, angel or not. They were equal-opportunity con artists with moral compasses guided by greed.

The other point of access would have been the bar. In addition to Colin, the two witches had been there, though I couldn't for the life of me remember seeing them. Considering I made it my business to keep track of everybody in the place in order to keep drinks full and shenanigans to a minimum, I was disappointed in myself.

I could understand missing the gorgon; Fiona and her crew had been down for lunch, so I would have assumed she was with them. The witches, on the other hand, were a mystery. I'd ask Blake about them, too, though Bob said they'd paid cash.

As always, the main building took my breath away a little bit. The entire resort was grand. It had been funded by a group of uber-wealthy interspecies investors who wanted a place to go where they could be themselves.

The first season was booked before the place was even built, so they pulled together an advisory committee that evaluated areas of improvement. As a result, they doubled the size and added extra charms allowing a wider array of species to enjoy the amenities—the dampening charm for the succubi and incubi being one of many.

The main hotel was twenty stories high and housed more than a thousand rooms, a casino, six pools, five conference areas, and a handful of restaurants and bars. In other words, Blake had his work cut out for him just keeping it running—thus the meticulous bookkeeping.

The main entrance was massive—probably a hundred yards across, split in two by a huge sphinx. She wasn't just for looks, either; she was yet another clever security measure. Since nobody except Blake, the security team, and a handful of employees could use teleportation into or out of the hotel, folks were much less likely to commit crimes if they knew they'd be eaten as soon as they dashed out the front doors.

"Hey, Margo," I said. Yes, the sphinx was a woman.

"Destiny!" she exclaimed, her stone face breaking into a smile. "What a pleasant surprise. I never see you up here anymore. I miss our late-night chats."

When I was the early waitress at the tiki, I'd wait outside for Blake to get off work, sitting between her paws and enjoying the ocean view. We'd talk about anything and everything.

"I know. I miss them, too. I close the tiki pretty much every night now, and since Blake and I ..." I pinched my lips together and huffed out a breath.

She nodded in sympathy. "I know, dear. It was all I could do not to eat the home-wrecking tart when she left that day. She deserved a few good chomps."

I patted her paw. "You're a good friend. I had to restrain myself, too."

"If it's any consolation, she hasn't been back, and I haven't seen him with another woman."

Lifting my shoulder, I said, "It doesn't really matter. I want him to be happy, but it just can't be with me."

She gave me the side-eye. "Don't forget who you're talking to, young lady."

Oh yeah, she saw into the hearts of all, whether they were beating or not.

I straightened my shoulders. "Well, I figure if I say it enough, one of these days it'll be true."

She clucked and shook her head. "Enough with the unpleasantness. To what do I owe the pleasure?"

"Well, it's actually another bit of unpleasantness, at least from a legal standpoint. I assume you heard Cass was murdered."

She dipped her head, and some sand cascaded to the ground around her. Even though she was stone, I'd always felt bad for her when the occasional high wind would blow sand in her face.

"I did," she said. "Nasty business, that. Bad for the resort, too. If we don't solve it quickly, it'll be a PR nightmare."

"Did you sense anything odd yesterday or in the past few days?"

She pulled in a deep breath. "No, but since they started selling day passes online, not everybody comes through here now." She paused. "There was something odd a few days ago with those gargoyles Cass hangs out with. They met with an incubus right over there, and not one of the good ones, either. Something changed hands, but it was too small for me to tell what, then the incubus went that way"—she motioned with her head to the south entrance—"and on their way past me, one of them said they were glad they weren't going to have to deal with Cass much longer. Called him a fool who'd gotten what he deserved."

I frowned. "Do you think it could have been the essence?"

She puckered her lips, thinking. "I suppose it could have been, but I can't say for sure."

So the gargoyles were at the top of my list, but they weren't the only ones.

"What about a werewolf named Colin Moore?"

"Hmm," she said, scrunching her forehead. "Moore. Handsome devil? Hair just a bit too long?"

"That's him. He threatened Cass not long before he keeled over."

"Yes," she said gently, inclining her head a little, "but so did you. If everybody that ever threatened that hideous man were a suspect, the investigation would be sunk."

I thought belatedly about Fiona. "You're right, I guess. Fiona threatened to turn him to stone because he was being a jerk to me."

Margo smiled. "I do love that woman. She comes out and talks to me some nights while she's here. She can relax around me and let her hair down, literally, since I'm already stone."

"Yeah, Fiona's great. Speaking of," I said, "have there been any lone gorgons, lately?"

"Actually, yes. Once checked in yesterday. She's a hotel inspector, so this trip is a mix of business and pleasure." She cringed a little. "You didn't hear that from me. Now that I think about it, she's probably a mystery guest."

I groaned and made a mental note to tell Bob and Elena. Mystery guests were the pits. Either the hotel or somebody from the council would send somebody in periodically in the guise of a guest. The person would stay a few days, use as many of the amenities as possible, then score each one.

Personally, I thought it was dirty pool, especially if the shopper had never worked in the industry, but I was just a peon.

"So probably not the murderer," I concluded.

Margo lifted a shoulder. "I'd say no. She doesn't strike me as the brightest bulb, and I didn't pick up any murder in her heart. She does have a mean-girl streak, though, and a heaping dose of rookie-level pettiness."

Her biggest gift—or mixed blessing, as she called it—was seeing the sins in a person's heart. I think it's why she tended to cut Blake a break. She knew he sincerely didn't intend to do anything wrong. Yet he did, intentionally or not.

"Anybody else you want to know about?" she asked.

"A couple of witches. Bob said they looked youngish, but you and I both know that doesn't mean anything."

"Sorry, sweetie. There are at least a hundred witches here right now. They're having a convention starting tomorrow, and many of them came early."

"Thanks for your help anyway," I said.

"No problem," she said. "Come back and see me more often. It gets lonely up here." A shadow crossed her face. "Des?"

"Yeah, Margo?"

"When you have to make a choice, have faith."

"General advice or specific?" I asked. Despite the cloak of humanity, she was a sphinx. Riddles were her thing, and she often saw the future, at least in snippets.

"Both," she said, smiling before she turned back toward the ocean and faded back into a statue again.

With a final pat to her toe, I stood and headed to see Blake. At least I'd managed to eliminate the gorgon. The field was narrower by one.

CHAPTER ELEVEN

I TOOK MY TIME WANDERING through the bottom floor of the hotel on my way to the elevators that would take me to Blake's penthouse office. I wasn't sure what I was going to say to him, and the last time I'd been in there was when he'd told me what he'd done. I'd had to walk past *her* on my way out, and it wasn't a memory I wanted to rehash.

Though there was a mishmash of everything from beachy souvenir shops to chic restaurants, everything somehow worked. Even though I'd been there for almost four years, I still got the festive, vacationy feel when I walked through, and it calmed me. I picked up a new pair of flip-flops from one of the shops, then womanned up and headed toward the bank of elevators.

Turns out, I didn't make it to his office. I'd just pushed the *up* button when the doors a couple elevators to my left slid open, and Blake stepped out. He was laughing with a woman that fit the description of one of the pair Bob had seen at the bar.

The smile slid off his face as they stopped in front of me.

"Destiny, hey!" he said, glancing back and forth between me and Ms. Perfect.

My gaze slid to the cute brunette next to him as I reached deep and pasted on my best *don't give a shit* look. She was dressed in jeans and a T-shirt, but somehow she made it look classy. I felt self-conscious in my

50

cutoffs and tank and wished I'd taken the time to at least put on some eyeliner.

He recovered first and started to make the introduction.

The hole in the floor I'd been wishing for appeared in the form of the elevator doors sliding open in front of me.

I smiled and pointed. "I'd love to stay and chat, but Fiona called and needs my help with something."

Trying not to be obvious, I jabbed the *close* button on the panel and picked a random floor.

I leaned against the brass rail at the back of the cabin and pulled in a couple deep breaths, willing my heart not to pound out of my chest. That could have gone better, but I supposed it was bound to happen sometime.

The elevator slowed then stopped, and I glanced above the door to see where I was at. The thirteenth floor. Weird, because that was my lucky number. I guess it was the universe saying *you're welcome for the quick save.*

The doors slid open before I could hit the *down* button again, and who to my wondering eyes should appear but Mr. Colin Moore himself. Well, well, I thought, stepping aside. I flashed him the distant, *strangers in an elevator* smile and clasped my hands behind me as he reached for the panel.

"What floor?" he asked.

"Oh. Uh, ground, please."

He punched the button then stepped back and mirrored my stance on the other side of the cabin. Somehow, it seemed like he was taking up a lot more of the space than I was.

Seeing as how I hadn't heard him say a peep the entire time he'd been there, I was surprised when he cleared his throat and spoke.

"Destiny, right? From the tiki?"

"Yeah," I said, glancing at him. "I've seen you there. And you are?" I figured he didn't need to know I already knew who he was.

One side of his mouth tipped up in a wry half smile, though he kept his eyes straight ahead. "Colin. Colin Moore."

"So, Colin Moore, what brings you to our delightful beach getaway?" I kept my gaze trained straight ahead too. Two could play the calm, cool, and collected game.

"A mix of business and pleasure," he answered, turning his head to look at me sideways. "And what brings you to it?"

I barked out a laugh. "Oh, you know. The usual. I got bored jet setting and decided to come down here and pretend to waitress for a couple years. I figured slummin' it would be a gas. Plus, I'm a sucker for the shoes and apron."

For the first time, I got to see that smile I'd imagined half a dozen times over the last week, and it looked even better on him than I could have guessed. I smiled back, even while the logical part of my brain was trying to tell the part that controlled the girly bits that he might be a murderer.

To be fair, though, that would pretty much make him my type. The guy I'd gone out with—twice—before Blake hadn't been quite that bad, but only because he lacked motivation. He preferred to snatch purses off little old ladies, a fun fact about himself that he left off the "about me" section of his Facebook.

I found out the hard way when he tried to pay for our dinner with a credit card belonging to a woman who had apparently reported it stolen. He left in cuffs, and I got stuck with the bill. At least we'd decided to skip dessert.

The elevator jolted to a stop, and the doors slid open. I took a deep breath, hoping Blake and Ms. Perfect had left the vicinity. My anxiety level spiked a little, but I figured Fate surely wouldn't bitch-slap me twice in the same hour. I was correct.

He turned toward the front of the building and continued by my side, matching my pace.

"Are you going back to the tiki?" he asked as we stepped outside.

"I am, but I'm off. I was just going to check in on things."

Day was slipping into evening, and the sun hovered just over the water, spreading waves of brilliant violets, pinks, and oranges across the horizon. The positioning of the entrance wasn't accidental, and the ocean view never failed to take my breath away every time I stepped outside, no matter what time of day it was.

The colors were outstanding even for the Enchanted Coast, and I stumbled, sucking in a breath when I saw the HD display of colors stretched across the sky.

Colin slowed too and gave a low whistle. "Wow. That right there makes the whole trip worth it."

"I joked about the shoes and apron, but if I have to work, why would I pick anywhere else?"

The faintest of breezes kicked up, and the smell of his cologne—a clean, breezy scent that mimicked the ocean air—wafted over to me, almost making my mouth water. I wished much more fervently than before that I'd bothered a little more with my appearance.

He moved a few inches closer to me, and I couldn't decide if it was intentional or if he was just taking in the astounding display and had shifted his weight to get comfortable. I kicked myself a little because my goofy libido hoped he did it on purpose.

We were standing beside Margo, who shifted ever so slightly to look at Colin then give me a wink before turning her face back toward the water. I rolled my eyes then shuffled over a little and hopped up onto her pedestal, settling in to watch the show. It was my favorite spot on the whole resort, both because of the view and because of Margo.

"You go ahead," I told Colin, "I'm gonna stay here and watch the sunset."

He tilted his head, examining me, and his gaze flickered to my legs before he jerked it back to my face. "Do you mind if I join you?"

On impulse, I shrugged and scooched over, patting the space beside me. "Not at all. I even saved you a seat."

I knew I should be taking advantage of the situation to ask him some questions, but there was just something about a sunset over the Gulf of Mexico that demanded your whole attention. The colors grew more brilliant as the edge of the sun slipped behind the horizon.

A few minutes later, the final bit slipped out of sight, followed by a slight green blink. I smiled, wondering if he knew how rare it was to witness that. No magic on earth could force it to happen; it was all on nature.

He took a deep breath beside me, and when I chanced a look, he was smiling again.

"No matter how old I get, an ocean sunset never gets old," he said.

"I know. Definitely a perk of the job." I knew I should push off the pedestal and go check on Bob, but I hated to break the moment. A group of young witches ran by, streaming sparklers behind them, doing it for me.

Reality crashed back, and he cleared his throat. "I guess we should head down to the tiki," he said, a note of regret in his voice.

"I guess so," I replied, pushing off the pedestal.

He followed suit, and when I looked back to wave to Margo, she was smirking just a little bit.

CHAPTER TWELVE

I WAS TRYING TO THINK of a way to broach the whole Cassiel thing when he did it for me.

"Any progress on the murder?"

My sense of humor ran toward the bizarre when I was nervous, and I huffed out a little laugh. "I'm pretty sure the murder progressed exactly as planned," I said. "It's the investigation that could use some help."

He furrowed his brow at me, and I wished I could pull the words back, until he laughed. "Semantics," he said. "As an attorney, I can appreciate that."

"You're a lawyer?" For some reason, that surprised me, probably because my first guess had been assassin. Though to be fair, some of the skill sets were similar.

"Sort of," he answered and left it at that.

I couldn't resist. "So how did you know Cass?"

He stuffed his hands into the pockets of his khaki shorts. "I wondered when you were going to come around to that. Or *if* you were."

"You brought it up," I reminded him, stepping over a melting ice cream in the sand.

"Fair enough. I didn't know Cass, per se, and my business with him was confidential, but I didn't kill him."

"Well, that clears everything right up, then. You're off the list."

He cocked a brow at me. "I didn't know I was *on* it."

I heaved a sigh. "It's nothing personal. As far as I'm concerned, there are several suspects."

"And you're at the top of the list."

It grated, but only because it was true. I did my best to tamp down my irritation. "So I've been told. But I'm the only one I know for a fact didn't do it."

"If it makes you feel any better, you don't strike me as the poisoning type."

I snorted. "You've got that right. I'm more of a *crime of passion* type girl. If I'd done it, it would have been much messier and more painful."

Another grin flashed across his face, and I found myself wanting to see more of it. It tickled through the back of my brain that the fact I was so attracted to him was probably more evidence against him.

"I'd have to agree with you," he said. "Poisoning's too sneaky for you. You strike me as the type who'd want him to see it coming."

"Well when you put it like that, it just sounds mean." That didn't mean he wasn't right, though.

"So tell me why I should believe you didn't kill him," I said. We were cresting the last rise before the tiki, and I was a little disappointed the walk was over.

"Do I strike you as the type to poison somebody?"

I examined him for a minute, rubbing my chin. "Hm. I don't know. It's not werewolf style, but you're also a lawyer, so until I'm sure, I'm not leaving any open drinks alone with you."

He laughed. "That's wise of you. Unnecessary, but wise."

Bob raised a brow at me when we popped around the corner, and it reminded me of how taciturn Colin had been all week.

"So what's your beef with Bob? The poor guy's been trying to entertain you all week, and you haven't cracked so much as a smile."

He sighed. "I know. I've had a lot on my mind. If you had any idea why I was here, you'd understand."

"Well, since you're not willing to share that information, be nice to him. He's a good guy."

"Yes ma'am," he said.

He went to the bar, and I watched to make sure he made good on his word. When he greeted Bob and started making small talk like a normal person would, I turned toward the patio. Stan wasn't there, which was surprising. Cyri and Aiden were walking along the beach, and the gorgons had built a bonfire a little farther down, right before the magical border that kept humans out and the resort invisible.

From the other side, it just looked like cliffs jutting out of the sand, making the way impassable. No confusion spells or repulsion spells necessary. Simple yet brilliant; it had been one of Michael's ideas.

The thought of him brought back the events of the afternoon.

Tempest curled around my feet.

Your mood just went from hero to zero, she said, and I was glad she was keeping it private rather than speaking out loud.

I explained what had happened.

I'm sorry, she thought, rubbing her head on my leg. *Too bad he didn't see you with the hottie over there. I thought we had him on the suspect list, though.*

We do.

I sighed. *It's complicated. He's nice and funny. But I can't rule him out, at least until I know what his business was with Cass.*

Shame. He sure is somethin' to look at.

I couldn't argue with that.

Either people had partied themselves out the night before or were entertaining themselves in the main bars up at the hotel, because it was quiet. A few tables were having dinner, and Bob had a handful of folks at the bar, but that was it. Elena had things under control, so I slipped into the office to do payroll, Tempest on my heels. It was quick and easy, thanks to automation rather than magic, and I had it done in no time.

"Did Michael call back?" Tempe asked, running her claws through the fluff on her tail.

"Not yet," I said, checking my phone for the hundredth time just to be sure.

"We can't just sit around here and wait for them to come get you," she said, hopping onto my desktop. "You're resilient, but death isn't really something you come back from." She paused, then added, "Well, you can, obviously, but not with a body. And lemme tell ya, it's bad enough not having thumbs!"

"I'm aware." I scowled at her and pulled the payroll backup paperwork from under her fluffy butt. "But what else is there to do?"

"You could always talk your werewolf friend out there into escorting us to see him."

"Absolutely not," I told her, then made a quick decision. "But I am going to go have dinner with him. I need to find out what he's hiding. If Michael doesn't call back by tomorrow morning, we'll come up with something."

CHAPTER THIRTEEN

I SLID ONTO THE STOOL beside Colin. "So, what's a nice werewolf like you doing in a place like this?"

He rolled his eyes. "Sitting here awash in disappointment that a really cute witch would throw such a cheesy pickup line at me."

"It worked, didn't it?"

"Sadly, yes. Either you put some mojo on it, or I need to socialize more."

Bob wiped off the bar in front of me and tossed down a coaster. "Lime water or beer?"

"Beer, please, and a grilled cheese with bacon and tomato." Just the thought of the cheesy, bacony deliciousness made my mouth water.

Colin raised a brow. "No *salad, squeeze of lemon, hold the dressing*?"

"Oh, hell no," I said. "I prefer salads exactly where they were meant to go—on top of a burger."

He grinned, and for the first time ever, I saw the incorrigible gleam I was used to seeing in the eyes of werewolves. "My kinda girl."

Bob laughed. "Better hold off on that. She's not kidding. I tried to sneak a fry off her plate once and about took an elbow to the nose. She doesn't play."

"In my defense, I was raised with four brothers and an older sister, and two of my werewolf cousins were there half the time, too," I said. "I learned early to throw an elbow if I didn't want to starve."

Colin about choked on his beer. "Did you say you have werewolf cousins? As in, blood relatives?"

"Yeah," I said, narrowing my eyes. Many paranormals frowned on mixed-species relationships, and I was about to throw down. I loved my oddball family. "I have five werewolf first cousins. One of them, Cori, is half witch, half were, *and* is alpha of her regional pack, and sheriff, too."

His eyebrows shot up. "Oh wow. I know your family. But just so you know, I was only surprised, not judging."

I realized I was probably being a little too sensitive, so I changed the subject. "I have to say, you've done a complete one-eighty today. What gives? Two days ago, you were broody and frowny, and now you're, well, not."

He pulled in a deep breath. "A couple things. I was wrapping up a huge case for a client. I really needed to be there to handle it, but since I couldn't, I had to do it online. It didn't start well, and it didn't get any better as it went."

He glanced at Bob. "Thus the failure to laugh at your mostly funny jokes. The one about the unicorn and the cyclops in the bar though? Horrible, man."

I smothered a laugh. That was Bob's favorite joke, but Colin was right. It was bad.

Bob scowled. "You were probably so buried in work, you just didn't hear it right."

"Oh no, I heard it. It was so bad my beer went flat. But the one about the priest, the rabbi, and the merman? Priceless."

That put the smile back on Bob's face. "Yeah, that's one of the ones you actually half smiled at."

Tempest hopped up on the cooler in front of Bob and introduced herself. Out loud. I cocked a brow at her.

"What? I can speak whenever I want, but it's exhausting hearing the oohing and ahing. It's bad enough when I *don't* speak, but Lord almighty, every time I open my mouth, it's like nobody's ever heard a talkin' fox from the South. I kinda wanna punch 'em in the throat. Or bite them on the calf."

Colin glanced at me. "Your familiar, I assume?"

Tempest scowled at him. "See what I mean? I'm *right* here."

"She's even meaner than Destiny," Bob told him. "I never thought I'd be afraid of a twenty-pound anything, but Tempest lives up to her name."

Our food arrived, saving us from any more ranting. Tempe and I were alike in more ways than one. I gave her a quarter of my sandwich and a few fries, and we settled into the business of eating.

I cringed a little when Colin offered her a couple onion rings, because onions gave her gas. When it came to flatulence, that little fox could give a skunk ape a run for his money. I glared at her, but she just smirked and popped one of them into her mouth. She found it hilarious when she gassed me out of our room.

While we munched, we discussed the murder in general, gossipy terms until he asked about the gargoyles.

"I don't know," I said. "They started coming around a couple months ago. They show up every couple of weeks, and Cass covers whatever they want. They're rude, crude, not too bright. Not to give him too much credit, but I was surprised Cass had anything to do with them. He thought he was better than everybody and didn't bother to hide it."

"Who are they?" he asked.

I lifted a shoulder. "No clue. I don't think I ever heard him call them by name. Cass comped everything, so I've never run a credit card on them."

I thought hard on it for the next few minutes, then decided to share what Margo'd told me, though I left her name out of it.

"So do you think it was possible that's when the essence came in?" he asked.

"Maybe," I said. "As far as I know, Cass wasn't going anywhere, so that was an odd thing for them to say. I'm waiting to hear back from my brother. He ... has a finger on the pulse of the seedier side of our world."

He shifted his weight. Something passed over his face too quickly for me to catch it, but Bob said something before I could call him on it.

"Cass was just a bitter, angry bully all around," my lumbering friend said. "If he weren't an angel, I wouldn't be so surprised somebody helped him check out early."

"Yeah, the only people he actively avoided offending were other angels," I added. "But even then, he only managed that because he avoided them altogether whenever they'd stop by."

Bob placed a glass of lime water in front of me. "She's right. The resort founders came as a group a few years ago just to check on things and brought their wives and kids. Cass remembered all of a sudden that he had important business somewhere off-resort, and I suspect it's because one of them was Arariel."

In case you're not up on your angels, Arariel is the Angel of Water, and he liked to pop in every couple of months. The resort was a pet project of his. I'd been more than a little intimidated the first time I'd heard he was coming. I mean, hello—angel. Not like disgraced-angel Cass but a full-fledged member of the winged super-society.

Despite what you may have heard, angels are neither inherently good nor evil, nor are they perfect—Cass was proof of that.

But the selection process for those positions had been rigorous, unanimous decisions made by the entire bank of existing angels. Only a few that I knew of had gotten on the naughty list, so I wasn't sure how Cass had managed to scrape under the limbo stick in the very beginning.

Colin crinkled his brow, confused. "But Arariel is awesome. He's the one who worked with the sea folks to get the water borders up for the resort."

Just like there were mirages used to keep non-magical people from entering via land, there were water and air boundaries, too. Those charms were much more intricate than the cliff mirages.

I laughed, thinking back to when I was still a noob at the resort. "The first time I heard Arariel and the other founders were coming, I was a train wreck. This really cool surfer guy had been there with some friends all week, and I got the news while I was waiting for Bob to make them all drinks. I made it to the cabana but was so rattled, I tripped over a cabana peg and the tray went flying. Thankfully, somebody was able to freeze it before the whole thing landed right in a girl's lap."

"Oh yeah," Bob said, chortling. "I remember that day. I've never seen you discombobulated."

Tempest snorted. "A hot mess is what she was. She's waited on every head of state from the Queen of England to the Queen of Faerie, yet one angel and a bunch of rich folks had her all in a tizzy."

Colin was smiling. "So did your customers get mad because you spilled their drinks?"

"Worse," I said. The memory still made me blush. "After I explained why I was such a klutz, they introduced themselves using first and last names. The surfer dude's name was Ari."

A look of dawning crossed his face. "Ari. Arariel. And his friends?"

I pressed my lips together and nodded. "Some of the other founders."

He laughed at me, and I couldn't help but smile back. "We'd had a blast all week, and I'd had no idea. They thought it was hilarious but took pity on me and laughed with me rather than at me. And they left me a huge tip. The point is, though, Cass took vacation that week. Ari comes around every couple of months, and whenever he does, Cass disappears."

Bob rubbed his chin. "You know, I'd forgotten about that day. I wonder how much it played into you getting your job back? If Ari stood up for you, I bet that really pissed Cass off."

He had a point. But oh well. Cass was his own worst enemy, and I refused to feel bad about it.

"Wait," I said, Colin's words sinking in. "How do you know Ari?"

He made a point of studying his plate. "I've met him a few times. Business." That seemed to be all I was gonna get, and I opted to leave it alone. I couldn't see how it mattered anyway.

We ate quietly for a few minutes, and I turned things over in my head. I'd asked Colin about his complete change of personality for a reason. He seemed like a nice guy—now—but it was a bit convenient that he only became Mr. Personality after the murder. As much as I wanted to give him the benefit of the doubt, that had rarely worked out for me.

My phone dinged with an incoming text from Michael when I was almost done eating.

M: We'd love to see you! Angelo's? 10 tomorrow?

I was surprised yet pleased. I loved my brother, but he wasn't exactly an exclamation-point kinda guy. Something more along the lines of *OK, tomorrow, 3pm, town square* would have been more up his alley. I didn't know if it was because his job had hardened him or he was just naturally a man of few words.

I figured it was probably a combination, because he'd been serious as a kid, too. Even when it came to practical jokes, he'd been sort of a buzzkill, because even on the rare occasion we managed to get one over on him, he never reacted. He just got even.

Regardless, he was my favorite brother because underneath the hard exterior, he was a marshmallow—and fiercely protective—at least when it came to me and Tempest. Even though Angelo's catered to a rough crowd—it was in Abaddon's Gate, after all—they had a great lasagna, so I was in.

D: See you then.

I relayed the message to Tempest via our mental link, and though she tried to play it cool, I knew she was excited.

I was a little disappointed when Colin quieted down a little then called it an early night. I picked through our conversation, trying to think of anything I may have said to offend him, but nothing jumped out at me.

When he left, I watched him go—don't judge—and was surprised to see Cass's merry band of gargoyles sitting at their regular table. They were staring at me intently, the light from the tiki torches flickering in their beady eyes. A sliver of ice slid down my spine. I went to the restroom, and when I came back, they were gone.

"Elena, how long were those gargoyles sitting there?"

She shrugged. "An hour or so. They came right after you sat down with yummy wolf boy." She wrinkled her nose. "It's a shame they smell like wet dogs, because some of them are F-I-N-E, fine."

I grinned, thankful for once that I didn't have that heightened sense of smell. I wish I had the hearing though, because maybe I'd have heard Cass's stony cronies.

My bigger worry, though, was had *they* heard *me*?

It was almost closing time, so I hopped up to help Bob and Elena clean up, telling them about the Gorgon spy so they'd be ready.

I was counting Bob's drawer when Blake's text notification sounded from my phone. I cringed and glanced around to make sure we were alone, because it wasn't exactly nice. I was relieved to see we were but dreaded opening it up. I pulled up my big-girl undies and did it anyway.

B: We need to talk

D: We really don't

B: C'mon Des. It's not what you think. It's work

D: Yeah OK Not my business. I'm going to Abaddon's Gate tomorrow, just FYI. I'm off but should be back by early afternoon to help if they need me.

B: Be careful. And we really do need to talk about work when you get back

D: Ok

I sighed and shoved the phone back into my pocket. That was a conversation I was looking forward to about as much as if I were having a tooth drilled.

CHAPTER
FOURTEEN

I SET MY ALARM FOR seven the next morning because if I had to leave the resort, I wanted to grab some supplies while I was out. We had plenty of stores on-site, but some things, including hair products and cold cereal—one third of my sustenance—were crazy expensive.

The more I thought about Michael's text, the more my bullshit meter screamed. He just wasn't that bubbly. I was going to feel like a real jerk if I turned out to be wrong, but Tempest agreed.

"As much as I'd like to think he was just sharin' the love, you and I both know he's not all sunshine and roses. I vote we browse the shop directly across the street and watch for him to get there first."

That was pretty specific, and I dug through my mind to figure out what was there. When I did, I laughed. "You just want chocolate-covered bacon."

ChocoLatte was a funky coffee and candy shop, owned and ran by a man who was both a chocolatier and a java connoisseur.

"Maybe," she said, "but you can't argue that it's not the best vantage point."

No, I could not.

"I'd like to stop and see Calamity, too." Calamity was her sister and was my friend Mila's familiar.

"Yeah, I was already planning to stop there. We haven't seen them in a while."

She smiled and trotted along beside me as I slung my backpack over my shoulder. We decided to walk to the north gate, which was the closest exit, rather than teleport. Nobody could teleport onto or away from the resort for security reasons.

The weather was beautiful, and between the sound of the ocean and the cry of the gulls, I was happy and peaceful. Only a little of the shine was dulled by the prospect that somebody may have set me up.

After all, Michael had one of the most secure lines on the planet. The PCIB didn't do anything by halves, so I knew he hadn't been hacked. Still, I couldn't shake the feeling something wasn't right, and I'd learned a long time ago never to ignore my gut.

The border was marked by red flags that fluttered in the breeze perpendicular to the water. It was see-through on our side; the flags were the only thing that gave it away. The only thing off was a door standing all by itself several yards above the high-tide line.

Much like an amusement park, you could leave any time you wanted, but you had to go through an exit, and you had to have a passcode to get back in. It was just another layer of security in place to protect all guests at the resort. There were emergency lockdown measures in place so that if need be—such as when Julius's skin came up missing—nobody could come or go from the resort.

There were two ways to exit the resort—you could simply walk through any of the gates if you wanted to teleport, or you could use the banks of ports (earth and sea) in the main hotel.

Those led to hundreds of locations around the world; there was a portal in almost every major city, including many in the oceans to accommodate water folks.

Employees had the luxury of simply porting to one of the gates and using our fingerprints to get back in. It sounds complicated, and I'm leaving out a lot of details and exceptions, but think of it as the magical version of Disneyland—one entrance, a few exits, many ways to get there, and you couldn't get in without a pass of some sort.

So, once I got to the exit, I crossed through the door, picked up Tempest, and pictured a little boutique a street over from ChocoLatte in Abaddon's Gate.

Though it was a dangerous place, Abaddon's Gate was like many cities struggling not to succumb to the darker side of its society. Because it was a city for paranormal people only, it was utterly unique. There were street vendors and shops that sold everything from designer clothes to real voodoo dolls, and like Bob said, if you knew where to look and who to ask, you could find almost anything.

I stopped at a street booth and picked up a new case for my cell to replace the one I'd broken a couple days before. My magic messed with it some, and the protective case kept my energy from screwing with it as much. Otherwise, I had to charge it a couple times a day, and reception would get spotty.

It only took a minute, but Tempest was squirming in my arms.

"Knock it off, or I'm going to set you down," I said, frowning as I tried to keep from dropping her. She hated to walk on the street because of the grime, and to be honest, I couldn't blame her. The streets seemed to always be wet, and the faint smell of stagnant water—among other scents—clung to the place.

The air was also scented with the aromas of fresh-baked bread, cooking meat, roasting veggies, candy, coffee, or whatever emanated from other shops in the immediate vicinity.

It wasn't even nine yet, so I decided to do some shopping. Like most people I knew, I bought the majority of my clothes at Walmart or Target. However, there were some things, such as the phone case that blocked paranormal energy, they just didn't carry.

Hair-care products were another great example. There was nothing in the human world strong enough to manage my curls, but I'd found a product made by a witch a couple streets over that kept the frizz away, no matter what, and she carried a non-clumping, waterproof mascara that actually lived up to its hype. You just can't do either one of those without at least a dab of magic.

Mila owned her own magical version of Bath and Body Works. She had candles, lotions, soaps, bath potions, liniments, supplements ... you name it. She was a hearth witch, and a damned good one. If you had a problem, physical or mental, chances were good she had something that would help.

The bell above her door was spelled to be cheerful; a light charm to lift your spirits when you came in. She said it worked both ways—she got to make people happy, and they weren't as prone to be hateful to her.

I couldn't even tell you how many times I'd wished for a bell like that when I'd had mean guests, but I would've probably whacked them with it rather than rung it for them. Despite what Blake and Bob seemed to think, I was not the poster child for patience, good will, temperance, or any other virtue. Well, maybe loyalty.

Before I pushed inside, a flicker of black caught my eye, and I swung my head to see a woman looking at a *Paranormal People* magazine at a stand across the street. As engrossed as she seemed to be, she'd been at a vendor across from the cell phone case booth, too.

I watched her for a minute, but she simply bought the magazine after chatting with the vendor for a second, then walked away.

Mila stood at the counter inside, smiling.

"Were you born in a barn?" she asked when I didn't move in straight away.

I shook myself and returned her smile, stepping in and letting the door slap shut behind me—I was just being paranoid.

Mila had a little faerie blood in her, and she got the genetics for perfect skin from them. Well, that and her products were the bomb. Her family was black Irish, so her porcelain skin was in stark contrast to her raven's-wing hair and brilliant, smiling blue eyes.

She rushed out from behind the counter and scooped me into a hug. "Where on earth have you been, girl? I haven't seen you in a coon's age."

I'd known Mila since we were kids, raised together like sisters in the hills of North Carolina. Her mama and mine had been best friends. She went home more than I did, so her accent was a little sharper, and it was good to hear a voice from home. How she'd ended up in Abaddon's Gate was a story for another time, but right at that moment, I was glad she was there.

"I know, and I'm sorry," I said. "I hardly ever leave the resort."

She pushed me back to arm's length and gave me a once-over. "Yeah, it must be such a cross to bear. That tan looks great on you, but lemme load you up on moisturizers and a couple products I have that'll let you tan but keep you from turning into a piece of leather before you're forty."

I laughed. "See, what would I do without you?"

"Turn into a raisin, that's what." She put her hand to her chin and puckered her lips. "Though if I just let nature take its course, I'll be the young-lookin' hottie at our reunions."

That was a joke—she was one of the most beautiful women I'd ever met, inside and out, so she already held that spot. Of course, I wasn't a hag myself. I wasn't vain, but I also wasn't ashamed of my game. Still ...

"Better load me up on the good stuff, then," I told her, still smiling. I reached into my bag. "I brought you something, too."

She squealed. "Ooh, what?"

I pulled out one of a set of shell necklaces I'd made. Each had a little conch pendant, and I'd imbued hers with the scent of sea air, then used a little sliver of my own magic to form a connection between the two so that when she touched it and thought of me, I'd know, and vice versa.

She swiped a tear after she clasped it around her neck, then fanned her face with her hands. "You! Now look, my mascara's going to run."

I reached into my pack and pulled out one of the two tubes of waterproof mascara I'd just bought, and she laughed, smacking me on the arm. "Shut up! What else do you have in there? A couple of princes, maybe?"

"Pfft, toads, more like it." I told her about Blake.

She chewed on her lip. "Do you think maybe it really was work? I mean, maybe she's a guest or a businessperson."

When she saw my raised brow, she backpedaled, like any good friend does. "You're right. What a ho, and he's a jerk!"

"Of course he's a jerk," Tempe sniffed as she strolled back into the front area of the shop with Calamity, her sister and Mila's familiar, "whether the girl's a ho or not. But she totally is."

"Total skank," Calamity agreed. "Who are we talkin' about?"

And that was why I loved all of them. We chatted for a while longer, and I left her shop laden down with goodies.

CHAPTER FIFTEEN

WHEN WE STEPPED OUT, I looked up and down the street for the woman, but she was gone. I wasn't one to jump at shadows, but an angel connected—however unwillingly—to me was dead and I was in Abaddon's Gate. Both reasons to err on the side of caution.

We made our way to ChocoLatte, and the smell of roasting coffee and melted chocolate was manna when we walked in. Charlie—yes, I recognize the unfortunate coincidence—greeted us, a cheerful smile beneath his beeswaxed handlebar mustache.

Tempe had already climbed to my shoulder and was checking out the different confections. He made the best truffles I'd ever eaten, and I already knew what she wanted, so I ordered for us, adding on as she pointed out a goodie I'd missed or I saw something I thought Bob, his wife, or Elena might like. At the last minute, I thought of Colin and threw an extra pound of chocolate-covered bacon on my order.

"Can you put that in a perma-cold bag, please? We're going to lunch, and I don't want them to melt." Another great thing about being magic.

I glanced outside and was happy to see that Michael was at our favorite patio table at Angelo's when my phone rang. I fished it out of my pocket and glanced at the screen as I stepped out of the shop, holding the door open so a large family with strollers and diaper bags could get in.

Speak of the devil, I thought, swiping to answer. "Hey brother," I said. "I just left ChocoLatte. I figured I'd wait here until you got to the restaurant, but I see you. I'll be there in five seconds."

There was silence on the other end, and I checked to make sure I hadn't dropped the call.

"You're in Abaddon's Gate?" he asked after a couple more seconds.

"Yeah," I said. "You told me to meet you at Angelo's for brunch. You're sitting on the patio. I see you." A cold finger slid down my spine, and the hair on the back of my neck stood up.

"No," he said, "I didn't. I just got your voicemail. I didn't get any texts from you, and I didn't send you any, and I'm not at Angelo's. Stop what you're doing and get back inside the chocolate shop right now. Don't leave until you hear from me."

I thought back to the weird feeling I had when he'd texted earlier.

"Wait, if that's not you, then who is it? Where are you?" I asked, but the line was already dead.

Tempest had heard the conversation. "Turn around now, Des. I don't think we should be on the street." She had her tail wrapped around my neck and was gripping me so hard with her claws that I could feel the tips of them even through the backpack strap.

Scrunching my forehead, I shoved my phone back into my pocket and pivoted back toward the shop. I swiveled my head back and forth, looking for anything suspicious. The thing was, everything there was a little shady. I caught a familiar flash of black out of the corner of my eye; the woman was striding across the street toward me, her arm out.

I'm no magical wimp, but I'm not stupid, either. We were in the middle of Abaddon's Gate, and it wasn't a place where angry fairy tale princesses threw unicorn poop and glitter at you. Plus, it was a powder keg. If one magical brawl broke out on the streets, all hell would break loose. I reached for my magic, but I wasn't at full steam because I was landlocked.

Still, I was no slouch and was pulling together a stunning spell—one I felt would cause the least disturbance—when somebody grabbed my arm from behind. Tempest growled and pivoted on my shoulder, and I let loose with the stunning spell toward the woman. My aim was dead on, and she fell forward onto the street.

I felt a surge of satisfaction when she landed facedown on the asphalt. That was gonna leave a mark.

The hold on my arm tightened and yanked, pulling me backward. "You need to come with me," he said, his voice gravelly.

Tempe's tail brushed against my chin as she growled again and flung herself toward my attacker. For just a second, the hold on my arm loosened, and I jerked free. I'd never seen the man before.

He used both hands to rip Tempest off his face and sling her to the ground, and rage tore through me when I heard her cry out. That was it.

Tempe had bought me just enough time that magic crackled between my fingertips. I was about a second away from raining a heaping helping of wrath on him, and damn the consequences. Nobody hurt my fox. Or manhandled me, for that matter.

Suddenly the man's face went slack, his eyes rolled back in his head, and he tilted forward, finally gaining momentum and landing with a satisfying crunch right on his face. Colin was standing behind him, holding an iron skillet he'd pulled off a nearby dwarf's cart.

I froze, without a clue as to what to do next. He lowered the skillet and took a step toward me, glancing over my shoulder as he did so. I noticed the Michael impersonator was gone from Angelo's and wondered if that was the guy Colin had just clocked. I wasn't willing to risk it.

Tempe had recovered and was standing by my side, hackles up and growling.

Do we trust him? I asked her.

Do we have a choice? Besides, we know the guy he took out was a threat, so right now ... enemy of our enemy?

Unless he's playing us.

She heaved a huge sigh. *I don't see where we have much choice, unless you want to take him down, too. The other two aren't gonna be out much longer. We need to move.*

A crowd had gathered, which was a bad thing in the Gate, and I stepped forward.

Back on my shoulder, please. I don't want to risk getting separated.

She hopped into my arms and resumed her position, and I pushed past Colin.

"Wait," he said. "I have a place. Follow me."

Making a judgment call, I did as he said. I didn't have a better idea, and I didn't know anybody other than Mila there, and I damned sure wasn't dragging them to her.

We darted up an alley, Colin looking back at us every few steps, then broke out onto a busy street behind a flower cart. People were bustling around us as usual, going about their business. We slowed to a walk, blending in.

"Wow," Colin said after a moment. "You stay busy on your days off."

I scowled at him.

"Too soon?"

"You think? Who were those people?" Now that I wasn't in obvious mortal danger, I was getting pissed.

"I don't know who that man was," he said, "but the woman may have been on your side. She was an angel's assistant."

"Say what?" I asked, unable to believe the mess the day had turned to.

"An angel's assistant. I'm not sure which one's, though."

"How do you even know that much? And why were you following me?" I asked, drawing my brows together.

He waved me off. "It doesn't matter how I know about the assistant. I was following you because I might have caught a peek at the text from your brother last night and didn't want you traipsing around the Gate by yourself." He ran his hand through his hair, rumpling it. "You weren't ever supposed to see me."

"Well," I said, realizing that no matter what, at least I wasn't dead or locked away somewhere, "you kinda failed at that part, but I can't complain, in the scheme of things."

"Speaking of your brother, where was he?"

Oh, crap. Michael. If he was already at ChocoLatte, he'd be freaking out. "It was a setup," I said, pulling my phone from my back pocket and hitting my brother's number.

He answered on the first ring. "Where are you?" he demanded.

"I'm safe," I said. "I'm a couple streets over, in front of"—I looked around for a landmark—"the Cracked Cauldron."

"Go in there. Go to the bar and tell the bartender you're my sister. I'll be there in five minutes."

"Okay, well I'm with somebody, so you—" I was going to tell him he didn't have to worry so much, but he interrupted me.

"You brought one of your beach friends to Abaddon's Gate?" He sounded irritated. "Fine. Take her with you. Just don't leave the place until I get there." Then he hung up.

Colin lifted a brow when I stared down at my blank phone. "Well, it looks like we're going to the Cracked Cauldron, then."

I took a deep breath and released it. "Indeed it does."

CHAPTER SIXTEEN

THE CRACKED CAULDRON was dark, but I was surprised at the appearance once my eyes adjusted to the dim lighting. A long, polished wood bar with a brass foot railing ran along one side, and booths lined the other. Tables sat in between, and in the back, there was a stage and dance floor. It looked just like any other dive bar I'd ever been in.

Rather than stop at the first stools, Colin chose ones at the far end and sat between me and the door. Considering I still wasn't sure of his motives, I didn't know whether that was a good thing or not, but he hadn't given me a reason to doubt him yet.

The bartender was a large, biker-looking dude with a full beard and a ready smile. "Welcome to the Cracked Cauldron. Name's Shane," he said as he slid two coasters in front of us.

"I'm Destiny," I said, then added, "My brother's Michael Maganti, and he'll be here in a minute." Michael had said to name-drop, so he must trust the place. Plus, if Colin turned out to be on team *let's kill Destiny*, the man looked like a good person to have on my side.

"So what's your poison, Destiny Maganti?" Shane asked.

I cringed a little at the unfortunate word choice, but it wasn't like he could have known. Or maybe he did; I'd learned never to take anything at face value in the Gate.

Figuring it wasn't exactly a lime-water kind of place, I decided to order something a little stronger. "What's on tap?"

He grinned. "Glad you asked. Our house tap is Summer Souls, a golden ale. Made in-house and has a mild hoppy flavor with a slightly fruity finish."

I raised a brow, surprised. "That's right up my alley, then. I'll do a pint."

Colin raised two fingers, indicating he'd take one, too. "And a menu, please."

The man turned and lumbered toward the beer taps, and I wondered what type of creature he was. Not human, because it was Abaddon's Gate, but I couldn't peg him, which meant he was probably a shifter.

Colin leaned toward me and confirmed my suspicions. "Bear shifter."

He returned with our beers, sliding a third in front of the empty seat beside me with a huge wink. "Yer brother'll be wantin' that when he gets here. No need to make him wait."

Sure enough, Michael pushed through the door a few seconds later, stepping immediately to the side so that his back was against the wall rather than the door. I felt a little bad that he did it without forethought, because that meant he was used to having his own back and to being in situations where he needed to.

He strode down the bar toward us, giving Colin the once-over, then said hello to me. "When you said you were with a friend, I thought you meant a girl."

"If you'd bothered to listen for five more seconds rather than cut me off and then hang up on me, you would have known. Colin Moore, this is my brother, Michael Maganti."

Rather than shake, they continued to take each other's measure.

"Oh for hell's sake. Both of you stand down. My beer's getting warm, but I don't want to turn my back in case the playground showdown turns to a shoving match. Michael, Colin saved my hide back there."

I glanced at the smug look that slid over the werewolf's features and added, "Though that doesn't mean I trust him. He's not given me a reason not to, though."

Michael gave a curt nod and slid onto the stool beside me, then downed a quarter of his beer in one drink. "Tell me what's going on," he said. "And try not to leave anything out."

Starting at the beginning, the day Cass was killed, I brought him up to speed.

He glanced at Colin. "Anything to add?"

"Yeah. The woman she knocked out in front of the chocolate shop was an angel's assistant."

Michael's jaw flexed, and he took another drink of his beer. "Why would an angel's assistant be after her?"

Colin shook his head. "I have no idea, except I know she's a suspect in Cassiel's murder."

My brother whipped his gaze to me. "Why are you a suspect?"

I shrugged. "As usual, he was being a dick and said he wished he could fire me. I told him I wished he'd drop dead. And a few minutes after I took him and his friends and hookers their drinks, he did."

Michael rolled his eyes. "Seriously, Destiny. Have you ever had a thought that didn't fall right from your brain to your mouth?"

"That's not fair," I said, scowling. "You know as well as I do, Cass hated me. And yes I have. I'm keeping quite a few of them trapped up there right now, for the good of advancing this conversation."

Tempe poked her head out of my lap, her fluffy little eyebrows drawn down. "I'm not. You're being a jerk. We were almost killed, or kidnapped, or something, and you need to be nice. Shame on you." She peered down at the floor. "And where's Rocky?"

Michael pointed his finger at her. "You're no better than she is. I thought as her familiar, you're supposed to be the voice of wisdom. Rocky's outside keeping guard."

Tempest narrowed her eyes at him. "I do my job, and I have her back. You realize if she's found guilty, she gets the death sentence, right? I figured if it took a trip to the Gate to get information, then it was worth the risk."

Michael sighed and slumped in his chair, the attitude draining from him. "I know, and I'm sorry. I should have been available."

"To her credit," Colin said, trying to put a positive spin on the situation, "there were several people who could have killed him besides her. As far as I'm concerned, she's the least likely suspect."

"Yeah," Michael said, scratching his stubble. Problem solving was his thing, and I was glad he switched into that mode and out of protective, bossy brother mode. "I don't like the snippet the sphinx overheard. Gargoyles aren't exactly known for loyalty, and there's something going on with them right now, though we haven't been able to figure out what."

He turned to me. "Can you have Blake pull the security footage of them? Maybe I'll recognize them. If not, I can run it through our database."

"Sure," I said, pulling out my phone. I wasn't going to risk another text going sideways, so I hit speed dial instead. While I waited for him to pick up, Colin ordered both of us a burger. I raised my brow at the assumption, but it's what I would have ordered anyway.

For once that day, luck was favoring me, sort of, and Blake picked up after a couple rings. Rather than engage him, I just said, "Michael wants to speak with you," and handed the phone over.

He told Blake what he needed then rattled off a secure number. "And if you have any footage of the two witches who were at the bar when the drinks were vulnerable, send that, too." He listened for a minute and hung up.

"He's pulling it up and sending it to me now," Michael said.

The guys ordered another beer, and it wasn't long before our burgers came out.

"I didn't hear you order anything," I said to my brother as Tempe climbed off my shoulder and onto the bar.

Shane smiled and slung his bar towel over his shoulder. "He didn't have to. In the five years I've known him, he's never ordered anything other than that right there."

Michael gave him a half smile as he squeezed ketchup onto his plate. "If it ain't broke, don't fix it."

It was one of the few times he let his Southern roots slip through, and I smiled, glad to catch a glimpse of the old him.

We were halfway through lunch when his phone chimed. He glanced down at it, then nodded to us. "It's the video."

I scooched closer because I wanted to see the witches. As luck would have it, there was a plant blocking the part of the bar where the drinks were sitting, and I made a mental note to remedy that as soon as I got back.

It cleared the witches, a couple of giggly chicks who ordered layered frozen drinks. I disliked them on principle but had to rule them out as suspects. Unfortunately, the plant was blocking where Colin had been sitting, too, so he was not in the clear.

"What about the video of the gargoyles?" Colin asked. We were both hovered over Michael, one of us watching over each shoulder.

Michael pulled up the next video. It showed me delivering them, then the exchange between Cass and me. I had to admit, the look of disdain on my face as I left the table didn't do anything to aid my cause.

He froze it on the next frame, the one that showed all three of the gargoyles' faces clearly. Michael jabbed a finger at the screen, pointing at the middle gargoyle.

"I don't recognize the other two for sure, but that one's been hanging around the Brass Tack, an antique store that's a front for the gargoyle faction in town. Money laundering, stolen goods, gambling, loan sharking."

"So he'd have access to death essence, then," Colin said.

Michael nodded. "Whether he's got the pull and the cash to get it is another question, but I have no doubt that crew could get whatever they wanted."

"So," Tempest said, stuffing one of Michael's tater tots into her mouth, "We've narrowed it down to three, then, and two of them are sitting right here." She looked back and forth between Colin and me, then appraised him, head tilted. She had her own special kind of magic, but she didn't let on what she saw.

"I say we go home," she said, turning to me. "You have no business chasing after gangster gargoyles in the armpit of the supernatural world. Your brother can do that."

She turned to Colin. "As far as you're concerned, you need to figure out where your loyalties lie. You're holding back. I don't know what, but you know more than you're saying."

CHAPTER
SEVENTEEN

ONCE WE WERE OUTSIDE the Cracked Cauldron, I figured Michael would go his way and we'd go ours. Colin said he had some business to take care of, but I was surprised when Michael turned in the same direction as I did. I shouldn't have been though; as protective of me as he was, I should have figured he'd see me home safely.

He led me into an empty alley, glanced around, and held out his hand. I scooped up Tempe, and Rocky leaned against Michael's leg.

"C'mon," he said. "We'll go together."

I furrowed my brow. "I've been porting since I was twelve," I said. "I think I can manage."

Rather than argue with me, he scooped up my hand, grinned, and the next thing I knew, we were standing outside the north border of the resort.

"See? How hard was that?" he said once I regained my balance.

"Not hard at all, which is why I would have been fine doing it myself," I said, hefting my backpack into a better position.

Michael hadn't let go of my hand, and he squeezed it.

"Destiny, please let me handle this. And don't be alone with the werewolf until we figure out what he's hiding. For me?"

I sighed. To be honest, I wasn't sure where to go from there anyway.

"Okay," I said, "but I'll keep watch for them around here. I have a feeling Cass wasn't the end of it."

"Fair enough," he said, pulling me into a one-armed hug. "Just don't leave the resort."

"Yes, Dad."

He shoved me toward the door, marked by two boulders on either side of it. To a human, it would just look like a couple big rocks against the cliff among a ton of other big rocks. He crossed his arms and waited as I placed my palm against the cliff and didn't move as I stepped through.

I turned back to him after it swung shut behind me, and he gave a general wave in my direction; he could no longer see me. I could see him, though, as he snapped his fingers and disappeared.

Tempe jumped down from my shoulders, watching the boys leave. Her brow was furrowed in concern. "I worry about them. They seem darker every time we see them."

"Yeah, me too," I said, stepping onto the path that led back to the resort.

"I just hope my troubles don't get him killed."

I used the time it took to get back to the resort to mentally organize the puzzle pieces I had. Some of them worked, but most of them were just random parts of a picture I couldn't see.

What would a gargoyle gain from killing an angel, and what prize was big enough to make it worth the risk?

Why was an angel's assistant, whatever that was, following me? I tried to puzzle out the expression on her face when she was crossing the street toward me. She'd had her hand out and had looked determined. But determined to what? Kill me or protect me from the guy who grabbed me from behind?

Michael'd been miffed that we hadn't tied the guy up or restrained him in some other way so he could have questioned him, but after I explained that things were turning ugly, he got over it. He, of all people, knew how fast the fire could spread in that area of town.

I didn't say anything, but I wish I would have thought of it, too. Hindsight was twenty/twenty, though.

Dimitri, our second bartender, was behind the bar. It always amazed me how different the fleet-footed faerie was than Bob, yet they were both great bartenders. Whereas Bob tended to be laidback and rocked the whole relaxed, island vibe, Dimitri was the life of the party, kickin' it to Buffett on the jukebox and tossing together fruity drink shooters for Elena to sell.

"Hey, Des," he said, smiling as he slid a citrus water toward me. He liked to use lemons, oranges, and limes. It gave it a different flavor than my usual, so it was a nice change.

"Hey, Dimitri," I answered, taking a big drink of my water. It was a scorcher, and I'd broken a sweat even though the walk from the border wasn't that far. "Has everything been okay?"

"Sure," he said, wiping down the bar. "Fiona and her crowd came down for lunch. This is their last day, so she said to tell you she'd see you next time."

He seemed to want to say something but was holding back.

"Anything else?" I prompted.

"Yeah," he drew in a deep breath, then released it. "Though I didn't know if I should mention it or not."

He was paying extraordinary attention to a nonexistent dirt spot on the bar. It only took me a second to figure out what he was trying to get around to—Blake and the brunette.

As badly as I wanted to think of her as a bimbo, I couldn't. She'd seemed classy, and the smile she'd given me when he tried to introduce us had been real. And I didn't want him to be alone and miserable forever. Much.

"Don't worry," I said. "I ran into them up at the resort yesterday."

"Phew." He blew a puff of air out through his cheeks. "I didn't want to be the one to tell you, but I didn't want it to blindside you, either."

"Oh, it did that, all right," I said. "I was on my way to his office when they came off the elevator together."

"Ouch," he said, then glanced at my outfit. "Please tell me you didn't go to see him dressed in anything like that and that you had some makeup on."

I glowered at him. "What's wrong with what I'm wearing?" It stung a little though, because he'd hit the nail on the head since I'd been wishing I'd taken the time to clean up, too.

"Then double ouch," he said, taking my protest as a confession.

"Yeah," I said, turning my back to him and propping my elbows on the bar behind me so I could gaze out over the water. "Double ouch, for sure."

CHAPTER EIGHTEEN

SINCE EVERYTHING WAS going well at the tiki, I figured I'd go to my cottage to put away my goodies. I'd spelled the backpack to hold everything I needed, but I didn't want to risk breaking the candles or having the lotions Mila'd given me leak all over the cereal I'd picked up. The candies were probably already squished beyond redemption, but that wouldn't stop me from plowing through them later.

I noticed a half-empty glass of water sitting on the bar a few stools down, the coaster under it soggy as though it had been there for a while. Stan made his way from the bathroom and pulled himself up on the stool rather than heading to his usual table.

I figured I must have mistaken the water for a vodka tonic, but Dimitri shook his head and whispered, "He's been sitting there like a kicked hellhound pup all day, sipping water and sighing a lot. He won't talk."

I was shocked when I took a closer look. His usually pristine white diaper—excuse me, loincloth—wasn't so pristine. It was a dingy gray with what I prayed were barbecue sauce stains on it.

His elbows were on the table, and his head hung forward between his shoulders. A good three days' worth of stubble covered his sunburned cheeks, and his curly blond hair was stringy and matted. In short, he looked like he'd hit rock bottom.

You're gonna have to do something about that before we go anywhere, Tempe said, and she was right.

I sighed and swung my backpack gently onto the nearest stool, then headed toward the hang-dog cherub, hoping he didn't burst into tears. I didn't deal well with those sorts of situations.

I tried to breathe through my mouth as I approached him; if I had to guess, he hadn't had a date with a bar of soap in at least three days. He pivoted his head sideways to look at me through bloodshot eyes when I patted him on the shoulder.

"Stan, my man. What's goin' on?"

He heaved a great sigh. "I'm obsolete, Des."

"Aw, Stan, that's not true."

"It is," he replied, and his eyes welled up. Ah crap; so much for no crying. Still, my heart went out to the poor guy.

"No, what you need to do is find a better class of people. Stop hangin' out in bars and following the dating websites. Those were great for a few years, but they've grown passé. People go there for kicks, not true love. Or most people do, anyway. Anyone lookin' for love on a barstool's fallen farther down the rung than you have."

"Really?" he asked, a trickle of hope in his voice. "You think finding some new workplaces would help?"

"I know they would. Try places like this. Or maybe those couples' retreats. Singles' cruises, though watch out for the players there. Outdoor events, sporting events. Anywhere people go to enjoy shared interests."

He was starting to perk up a little and reached forward for his glass. "Yeah, and maybe I should be a little more selective, too. For the last few decades, I've been going for quantity over quality."

I raised my brows and smiled. "See there? Another way to up your game. Those arrows are valuable. Don't dilute your product by firing them at just anybody. Do some research. Put a little effort into it."

Dimitri'd ghosted his way down the bar, and when he heard things going well, he chimed in. "And I'm sure there's a ton of work that needs done on the other end of the love spectrum, too."

Stan scrunched his brows together. "What do you mean?"

"We get couples in here all the time that have been married for decades or even centuries. They still love each other, but the romance is gone. A good power-up with a couple of those arrows is just what the doctor ordered."

"Oh," Stan breathed, his eyes lighting with realization. "You mean like follow-up appointments. Booster shots, so to speak."

"Exactly," Dimitri said, slapping his hand on the bar and adding a few ice cubes to Stan's glass.

Stan sucked the last of the water down and pushed off the stool. Tears pooled in his eyes again, but this time for a different reason.

"Thanks, guys!" he sniffed. "You don't know what you've done for me—I can't thank you enough. Now, I need to go put some love back in the air!"

He pulled me into a hug, mashing my face against his sweaty bare chest, and I did my best not to breathe.

Pushing me back to arm's length, he said, "You're the best! I really hope they don't give you the death sentence."

I furrowed my brow. "Uh, thanks?"

With a huge grin on his face and the sparkle back in his eye, he strode down the bar.

"Stan?" I called, wrinkling my nose.

"Yeah?" he asked over his shoulder.

"Shower before you do anything."

He raised his arm and sniffed, his face puckering. "Oh yeah. Good idea." He looked down his body and peered into the side of his drawers. "I could use a fresh loincloth, too."

"Too much information, buddy," I said, holding up my hand. "But don't be a stranger."

Dimitri shook his head as the invigorated cupid disappeared around the corner. "We have the strangest jobs."

"That we do, 'Tri. That we do."

I figured putting Cupid—or at least *a* cupid—back on track was enough work for one day, especially given I'd done my shopping, about had my hair yanked out by somebody bent on killing or maiming me, and found a great new dive bar. It was barely past noon, so I decided to take a bubble bath with some of the new goodies Mila'd given me, catch up on laundry, and watch some TV.

You know what they say about the best-laid plans.

CHAPTER NINETEEN

AS AN ON-SITE EMPLOYEE, I had my own cottage. The Enchanted Coast offered three different types of housing for folks who wanted to live there rather than commute: dorms, one-bedroom cottages, and houses for families only. There was plenty of dorm space, but cottages and houses were limited and divvied out according to seniority.

I'd lucked into mine when one of the managers had gotten married and moved into a house. It cost more than my standard board allotment, but not having to stare at somebody else's hair in the drain or share a sink while I brushed my teeth was worth whatever I had to pay, as far as I was concerned.

As a water witch, I wasn't much for growing things, but I'd picked up some tricks along the way when Mila's mom had given her lessons. I liked to cook, too, though baking was beyond me. I was more of a *dash of this and pinch of that* kind of girl, much to Tempe's chagrin. She loved pastries, but about the best I could manage were boxed brownies.

I waved my hand to undo the wards on my gate and was surprised when I didn't feel the little magical poof that happened when they dissipated. I paused.

"That's not right," Tempe said, the fur standing up on her back. "Are you sure you set them this morning?"

If I didn't, it would shock me because it was so ingrained that I did it automatically. I couldn't remember doing it specifically that morning though. I'd grabbed my coffee and had been lost in thought. Maybe I hadn't.

The door to the house was always spelled too, and when I released those wards a few feet before I reached it and nothing changed, I stopped in my tracks. I was a sitting duck where I was at, but there wasn't really a good hiding spot. It's not like I had a car or anything to hide behind.

Putting myself tight against the house was my best option. I'd be visible to anybody watching the house from the outside, but anybody inside wouldn't see me if they hadn't already.

I skittered to the side and forward, squatting down under my front window, then muttered a few words to erect a one-way mirror ward around just the cottage. That should take care of anybody watching from afar, but I could still see anybody approach.

Stay here. They'll be looking for somebody human-sized, Tempest thought, then moved toward the door before I could stop her.

She had her own pet door—or rather, familiar door, and she slunk toward it. I held my breath as she shot forward through it, praying she'd be okay. She was no magical wimp, but she was a long way from bulletproof.

Less than a minute later, she came back outside. "It's clear. Nobody's in there, though it does look like somebody searched the place. They didn't make a mess, but things have been moved."

I started to take down the mirror ward but changed my mind. I'd feel better leaving it up, even though it was technically against resort rules. Too bad—so was going through my house. Speaking of, I needed to call Blake and let him know what had happened.

He picked up on the third ring.

"Somebody broke into my cottage," I said without preamble.

"I know," he said.

I'd been about to tell him the story but clamped my mouth shut when he said that.

"You know," I said after taking a couple seconds to process it.

"Yeah. They showed up right after you called, demanding to see you. When I told them you were off today, they insisted on seeing your house, and they weren't exactly the people you say no to."

"What does that even mean?" I asked. Blake was a lot of things, but a wimp wasn't one of them.

"I mean, two of them were from the PCIB, and they were yes-sirring and no-sirring the other two men with them. And there was a blonde woman with a black eye that those two yes-ma'amed."

"A blonde woman? Tall? Trench coat, long hair? Looks like she eats nails for breakfast but wouldn't chip a nail while doing it?"

"That's a really weird way to describe her, but yeah."

"That's the woman who was following me in the Gate this morning. And the one I stunned. Since she wasn't rockin' a black eye then, that's probably on me. So what did they want?"

"They didn't say. I did insist on being there while they searched your place."

The magical world worked a little differently than the human one. Because it was easy to make evidence disappear in the blink of an eye, literally, search warrants weren't a requirement in criminal cases. That being said, probable cause was. It was a compromise most everybody, except criminals, of course, thought was fair.

So, that meant they thought they had probable cause to search my house.

My face flamed as I wondered if he'd seen the pictures of him with his eyes scratched out and little vulgar dialogue bubbles penned in. Oh well. Not my problem if he did.

"Thanks for that," I said, meaning it. Though I didn't have anything of real value, the thought of somebody pilfering through my undies drawer didn't sit well with me, and it was nice to know that at least somebody I trusted was there to keep things on the straight and narrow.

And yes, in a situation like that, I trusted him. As a matter of fact, unless it involved his lips, I trusted him implicitly.

"Did they take anything?"

"Not that I saw," he said, "but they were silent the entire time they were doing it. It was weird. One of them just stood in the middle of the room with his eyes shut like he was meditating the whole time. When the rest of them were finished, they looked at him, he nodded, and they left."

He nodded. What did that mean? Was he just saying he was finished, or was he saying he found something? No matter whether you're innocent or not, you're always a little guilty of something, and that naturally plays on your fears in a case like this.

And there was always the irrational fear that something benign to me could be stretched into something significant to them. People were convicted on circumstantial evidence all the time.

Or what if whoever did it planted something at my place? I mean, my wards were good, but I didn't go out of my way to reinforce them. Crime on the resort was minimal because most of us were friends, and Blake and crew vetted the crap out of everybody who applied. Still ...

"I wanna put extra wards up around my cottage," I said.

"Are they the same wards you've always used?" Meaning, did I still set them so he could come and go as he pleased. When we were together, it was a pain to make him wait for me to get home, so I'd just built the modification into the spell. When he admitted to swapping spit with Helena the Homewrecker, I'd switched back to the standard spells and maybe added a couple of boobie traps.

"No, but they can be."

He paused, and I got the awkward feeling that his feelings were hurt. But why on earth would he expect me *not* to change it?

"All right," he said. "Change them so that I have access, and I think it's a good idea to leave them up."

"Thanks. I'll change them now. And how did you get past them earlier?"

"That was all them. Just to let you know, though, they struggled with them a bit."

I smiled a little at that. At least I'd made them work for it.

"And Des? I need to talk to you about Lucy," he said.

"Who's Lucy?" I don't know why I was pretending; maybe I just wanted him to have to say it.

"The woman you saw me coming out of the elevator with."

"Oh, her. Yeah, it's no big deal."

"It kinda is," he said. "Be in my office tomorrow at noon, please."

"You're making it official?"

"Of course I'm making it official," he said, sounding confused. I wanted to throat-punch him. "Why wouldn't I?"

I opted to just stop fighting it and get it over with. "Fine. I'll see you in your office tomorrow at noon."

"Thank you. Oh, and Destiny?"

"Yeah?"

"I saw the pictures. I'm sorry I hurt you."

"Yeah," I said. "Me too."

CHAPTER TWENTY

I WENT THROUGH THE house and put things to rights, though there wasn't much disturbed. At least they'd been considerate enough not to trash the place. I called Michael, who picked up for once, and told him what had happened.

"Well, we know the woman's an angel's assistant, at least according to your friend. Two were PCIB guys, and I can find that out in a heartbeat. The other two stump me, though."

"Maybe the one was some sort of psychic, or energy tracer, or living X-ray machine or something."

He gave a dry laugh. "You covered a lot of ground there. I don't know, but I'll do my best to find out. 'Til then, don't leave the resort. Please. I may want to disembowel Blake for what he did to you, but I know he'll keep you safe."

That pissed me off a little. "If you remember, I was always better at self-defense spells than you were, and I'm a stronger witch by far than Blake is, even if he does brag about his levels. I'm pretty sure I'm capable of taking care of myself."

"Don't get your panties in a wad. I meant with the law. He's got some pull and can hopefully keep your neck out of the noose until we can figure this out. From what I've been hearing, the natives are getting restless. They want somebody's head on a pike."

"Oh," I said. Even though none of my brothers doubted my abilities, they did still tend to be overprotective big brothers. What they didn't understand was that just growing up with them had prepared me better for defending myself than any class could have. "Yeah. Staying alive to see this through is kinda a goal of mine. Speaking of, any luck with the gargoyle?"

"Not yet. But I did find out something about Colin Moore."

"Do tell," I said. "I've been trying to pin down his game since I met him. I don't feel like he's lying, per se, but he's not layin' it all out on the table, either."

"Right as always, little sister. He's an attorney, all right. But one of his biggest clients is—drumroll please—the DAB."

"Shut up!" I said, shocked. The DAB, or Divine Advisory Board, was the liaison between angels and deities and the rest of us peons. "What does a lawyer for them even do?"

"No clue, but I think it would be a good idea to find out."

My mind popped back to his sudden change in attitude. "Yeah, I think that would be a good idea, too. And I'd kinda like to know why he didn't bother to mention it, you know, seeing as how a member of his biggest corporate client ended up dead and stuff."

The hair rose on my arm—one of the warning signals from my ward. I looked out, and who should be standing outside of it but Mr. Angel Lawyer himself.

"I'm gonna let you go, Michael. It looks like I'm gonna get a chance to ask questions sooner rather than later. He's standing right outside my house."

"Text me when he leaves," he said.

"Will do, and let me know if you hear anything about the gargoyle," I said, then hung up and opened the ward so Colin could get in. He took a step backward when I did. I giggled when I realized what it must have looked like to him. One second, he's staring at himself; the next, he's looking into my yard and at my house.

"C'mon in," I yelled. "We need to talk."

He stepped through the space, then I closed it up again. He turned to look behind him and reached out to touch it. I didn't feel anything that time because I wasn't trying to keep anything in, just out. Of course, from inside, you couldn't even tell there was a ward in place. The view was the same as it always was.

"That's impressive," he said. "How much energy does it take to maintain it?"

"None," I said. "I'm a water witch. I set them to draw off the ocean. This close, it's a snap. Even inland, it's not a big deal. There's almost always extra energy of some sort in the air or ground."

I thought back to the one trip I'd taken to a major city. No water, no real plants to speak of, no breeze ... I didn't know how any witch could live there, but then again, I was raised in the country.

I didn't have a porch, which was one of the few things I didn't like about my cottage, so I invited him inside and motioned him toward the kitchen.

He looked around, then took a seat at my little glass-topped table.

"Tea or water," I asked. Though I drank water at work most of the time, I still held on to the sweet tea habit I'd had all my life when I was at home.

"Tea," he said.

"I just got off the phone with Michael," I said as I poured us each a glass. "He tells me you have some powerful clients. One in particular."

He pulled in a breath and huffed it out. "I was wondering how long it would take him to find that out."

I gave him a small half smile. "He's sharp, and he's connected. It doesn't take him long."

"In my defense, I wanted to tell you, but I'm bound by a nondisclosure agreement. Like, literally bound. I'm tongue-tied. I couldn't have told you if I'd wanted to."

"What about now that I already know?" I asked, taking a sip of my tea.

He lifted a shoulder. "Not sure. Nobody that isn't authorized has ever asked me anything, so I've never tested the boundaries of the NDA."

"What was your business with Cass?" I asked, testing the waters. Of course, even if he could tell me didn't mean he would.

He shook his head. "Client/attorney privilege. I'd tell you if I could, but I can't."

"You mean you physically can't, or you won't?" I didn't mean it as a jab; I was curious.

"I mean I won't," he answered, then looked at his glass. "That's some strong tea."

That earned a real smile; everybody who drank my tea said the same thing, but I couldn't stand it weak. "I'm from the South. It's the only way I know how to make it."

He rolled his eyes. "Good grief. I should have known. Where the tea is sweet and the witches are wicked."

"And don't you forget it either, buddy."

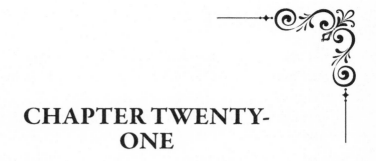

CHAPTER TWENTY-ONE

I DIDN'T ACCOMPLISH much the rest of the day, which was kind of my goal.

After we finished our tea, I asked if he wanted to go to the beach. The idea of rattling around the house doing various forms of nothing had lost its shine, and I wanted to get out.

"Don't you get sick of the beach, working and living here?" he asked.

"Are you crazy?" I asked, only half kidding. "I love it. There's just something about the water that's humbling. Plus, I'm allowed to do whatever I want in the hotel, too, as long as I *don't* do anything that could harm the reputation of the Enchanted Coast Resort or engage in any behavior criminal or otherwise that could cause legal liability or harm to the corporation, the brand, or the individual stockholders." I put most of that in air quotes.

He laughed. "As an attorney, I have to say that leaves quite a bit of gray area. How do you feel about gambling?" His eyes took on the gleam specific to lovers of the game. It surprised me because he didn't strike me as a risk taker.

"How do I feel about it? I feel like I could take your money at five-card and beat the pants off of you at blackjack."

He narrowed his eyes at me. "Is that because you're a witch and can cheat?"

"Oh, no," I said. "The whole casino is spelled against any kind of magical cheating. I have no idea how they managed it, but I couldn't cheat if I tried."

"What about counting cards?" he asked, curious.

I tilted my head. "I don't know. I'd assume there's something in place, but all I know for sure about is the magical enchantments."

"Then how about this—we spend a couple hours in the casino, then head to the tiki and spend some time in the water."

It occurred to me that he'd just mapped out my entire day. "Does this sudden desire for my company have anything to do with earlier?"

He shrugged. "It's about fifty-fifty. I think you don't have eyes in the back of your head and could use an extra set, but I also find myself enjoying hanging out with you."

Well, points for honesty, anyway.

Tempest only had to hear the word casino and she was ready to go. That little fox was a gambler through and through, and she was good at it, too.

She butted me with her head, pushing me to hurry. I didn't go up often because between working and hanging at the beach, it just wasn't something that held much appeal, so when I did want to go, she didn't give me a chance to change my mind.

I changed clothes and grabbed the beach bag on the way out the door—the one good thing about our resort was that, unlike many casinos, the only dress code was that you be actually dressed. There were even folks in damp bathing suits, so I didn't feel out of place in jean shorts.

We were almost to the casino before I remembered I'd told Michael I'd text him when Colin left. No need to scare him or have a hit put out on Colin, so I fired off a quick text to let him know I wasn't dead or in jail.

The casino was busier than I'd expected it to be, and after playing a few hands each of five-card and blackjack—and beating Colin more than I lost—I was starting to get claustrophobic. I looked around to see if Tempest was anywhere in sight and jolted when my eyes landed on Lucy, Blake's new squeeze.

I wondered if she worked there or if she was just vacationing and visiting him, then tried to push all thought of it clear out of my mind. The task became much easier when Colin bumped me with his shoulder.

"Everything okay?" he asked.

I tore my eyes off the pretty brunette and focused on the hot guy I was with. His blue eyes reflected concern and a little confusion. He'd noticed where I was looking. "Do you recognize her from somewhere? Do you think she's following you?"

After pulling in a deep breath and huffing it out, I shook my head. "Nope, it's not me she's following. C'mon. I could use some sunshine and surf."

Tempest was nowhere to be seen but answered as soon as I called to her through our link.

And I saw the woman you were staring at. Is that her?

Yeah, that's her. Let's just go.

The pool was back open when we got there and seemed to be the place to be. Cyri and Aiden were there, Bob was there with his wife and kids, and Amber and Dax had come up through the ocean channel, too. The pool was another genius idea and was one of the most popular features of the resort.

I waved at everybody and dropped my bag off on a lounge chair in the shady area but then headed to the beach. The pool would be great in a bit, but first I wanted to do a little communing.

The Gulf of Mexico didn't have big waves, but I was a water witch—that wasn't a problem. We kept a few surfboards in a storage locker, and I grabbed one while Tempest went into the bar and hopped into her customary spot in front of the fan. Colin reached around me and grabbed one a bit longer and followed me to the water.

"You surf?" I asked, surprised.

He shook his head. "Nope. Never been on a surfboard in my life."

"Then I'll be gentle," I said, closing my eyes and calling to the water. The waves increased in front of me, and I pushed out into the surf.

"Follow me," I said, grinning. "I'm sure you'll be a natural."

He so wasn't a natural, though he did give it his best shot. Even though he fell every time, he still came up laughing.

"C'mon there, Kahuna," I said after an hour or so. "Let's go grab something to drink and find some tamer entertainment, like hanging out with a couple of merfolks and a family of Sasquatches."

We were stepping out of the surf, laughing, when something sharp dug into the bottom of my foot. I instinctively shifted my weight, then lost my balance and bumped into him. He grabbed my shoulders to steady me, and I looked up to thank him.

Whatever I was going to say flew out of my brain as I found myself eye level with his generous mouth, still curved into a smile. I looked up into his eyes, and the smile slipped. His eyes went from ice blue to smoldering gray, and he leaned forward. I rose up on my toes to meet him.

As luck would have it, Tempest's voice sounded in my head, breaking the moment.

Destiny! Your phone's ringing, and it's Michael.

Okay, I'm coming. Answer it or tell Bob to. You have the worst timing ever, just so you know.

Or maybe I have the best. We still don't know what his deal is with the angels, so maybe sucking face with him isn't the best plan right now.

I patted him on the chest with a wry smile. "Duty calls."

"Lemme guess," he said as I pulled back. "Tempest."

I gave him a wry smile. "Ding, ding. Got it in one. Michael's calling. She's answering, but I need to go see what he has to say."

"He has the worst timing ever," he said, repeating what I'd just told Tempe.

"Yeah," I agreed, smiling. "I think it's the big brother gene. He has some kind of warning ward attached to my lips." I joked, but I couldn't help but think that maybe Tempe was right.

CHAPTER TWENTY-TWO

BOB WAS TALKING ON my phone when I got to the pool but said goodbye and handed it to me.

"Hey Michael, what's up?"

"What's up is that your boss was working with the gargoyles. We've captured some conversations where they were talking about Cass backing out of a deal and getting what he deserved."

"Any idea what?"

"No, but the other two gargoyles he was with are thieves and low-level thugs. Still, they have some deep connections with people who would be able to get the essence."

"Huh, so have you found anything new on the guy who attacked me? I don't understand where I'd fit into any of this. Cass and I were the exact opposite of bosom buddies," I said, noting that Colin was making a point to stand close enough to hear the conversation. Stupid werewolf hearing.

"Not yet. And I haven't figured out where werewolf boy fits in, either."

I muttered a quick muffling spell so that Colin wouldn't be able to hear what we were saying, then walked to the other side of the pool.

"He admitted to working with the angels but also says he's under a magical NDA. But then when I asked what his business was with Cass, he wouldn't say. Wouldn't, not couldn't. Claimed client privilege."

"Well, don't trust him. Angels are tricky and don't follow the same rules of logic that mortals do. I gotta go. I'll check back with you."

The line went dead, and I was left wondering how in the world I, a peon waitress by design, had managed to land myself in some kind of angel drama. When I was a kid, Mom used to tell me that I attracted more trouble than all of my brothers together, but this was ridiculous.

There was nothing I could do about it right that moment, though, so I tried to relax and enjoy my friends.

Bob's wife, Jolene, was from Tennessee and had packed fried chicken. The smell when she opened the basket made my stomach growl. Employees ate for free when we were on the clock, but if we were just hanging out on our off days, we only got a 10 percent discount, and that didn't apply to families.

Considering they had three kids who each ate more in one meal than I ate in two days, I understood why they chose to picnic rather than pay. We made good money, but not that good.

She invited us to eat with them, and I jumped on it. Fried chicken was my Achilles heel, and hers was every bit as good as my mom's, though I would never utter those words out loud, at least where my mom might hear it.

"So, I've been thinking," Bob said, waving a chicken leg. I had to stifle a giggle because the chicken looked more like a drumette in his baseball-mitt hand.

"Well there's a scary thought if ever there was one," Jolene said, bumping him with her elbow.

Watching the interplay between them made me both happy and sad at the same time. I was glad Bob was happy; nobody deserved it more than he did. But at the same time, less than a year ago, I'd thought that level of happiness was within my reach. I'd even tried to forgive Blake and get past it in the relationship because it was so out of character for him, but I just couldn't do it.

So, I found myself alone again.

"Ha-ha," he said. "Count yourself lucky I don't tend to put a lot of thought into things, woman. Have you met our kids?"

Jolene grinned. "Yeah, they're just like their father."

He snorted. "If I didn't know you better, I'd take that as an admission that you'd cheated on me with a demon. Three times."

His kids *were* a handful, but they were just rambunctious. Like Bob and Jolene, they had good hearts, plus, unlike Bob, Jolene cracked the whip.

"Let's hear it then, Boy Genius. What evil plot have you come up with now?" She took the sting out of her words by smiling as she handed him another piece of chicken and blopped more potato salad on his plate. Nothing says love like homemade potato salad.

"What if all this angel crap has nothing to do with Cass? I mean, it's not like he was a well-loved, upstanding member of our community. He treated everybody like dirt, and we have some powerful guests. And employees for that matter."

I'd thought about that, but most of our clients were upscale, and I couldn't think of a single one of them who seemed shady enough to pull something like that. Of course, he'd offended people on a daily basis, so that didn't mean he hadn't hit on somebody's wife or called somebody a dumbass one too many times.

"Maybe so," I said, shrugging and pushing my empty plate back. "He was an equal-opportunity dink of the highest order."

We tossed around some ideas about possible suspects, but nobody jumped out. In general, he preferred open disdain to picking fights, which meant he did his own thing and left us to deal with the riff-raff, even though many of said riff-raff were millionaires or better.

"Well, I think that's enough speculation and murder talk," Jolene said, digging a couple of pies out of the basket. "Apple or cherry?"

"Yes, please," Tempest replied as she finished off a chicken breast.

Bob laughed. "Little one, I don't know where you put it. You eat your weight in food every day."

She puffed herself up. "I'm a growing girl. It takes a lot of calories to keep Destiny out of trouble."

"Pfft," I said, "You're growing, all right. It about broke my back carrying you yesterday."

In truth, she hadn't gained a pound since she reached her full adult size, but Bob was right; she tore through the groceries. She'd eat sweets until she was sick, though.

"Just give her a sliver of each," I told Jolene. "We still have candy at the house, and I know she's going to get into it when we get home."

Tempe's eyes lit up. "Oh yeah. Chocolate-covered bacon."

By the time we finished eating, the sun was setting.

Full and content, I considered porting home but figured I should walk off some of the calories. I made Tempest walk, too, and Colin walked with us.

I invited him to stay for a movie and told myself it was for extra security. That was partly true, because even though I had complete confidence in my abilities, these were angels. I was many things. Stupid wasn't one of them. Plus, the idea that strangers had tromped through my house made it feel off to me.

If I were honest with myself, though, I also wanted to spend a little more time with him.

I'd given him the option of choosing the movie, but he'd declined. He just kept telling me that whatever I wanted to watch was good with him.

"Fine," I said. "*American Werewolf in London* it is, then."

He groaned. "You've gotta be kidding me. That movie is almost singlehandedly responsible for why werewolves have to stay locked in the closet. It's the same as if I asked you to watch *The Wizard of Oz*. I changed my mind. I'll help pick the movie."

I laughed because he was right. Don't get me wrong—I love me some Judy Garland, but there's no actress that could have made that movie good from a witch's standpoint. Plus, everybody knew the movie was cursed. Probably by a witch who'd read the script.

"So what about *Thor*?" I asked.

"Let's settle on *Avengers*. Then we both have eye candy as well as action."

"Deal." I made some microwave popcorn and broke out the candy, then settled onto the one end of the couch while he claimed the other.

Tempest settled between us, a piece of chocolate-covered bacon in each paw and we lost ourselves in gratuitous violence and destruction that wasn't aimed at me for a couple hours.

I'd drawn the line when Colin suggested sleeping on the couch. I had enough wards set on the place that, at the very least, I'd have enough warning to grab Tempe and port out if necessary. I was also ready to be alone. I needed to sort through my feelings and shove them in a box, at least until I figured out what his angle was.

He pulled his phone out of his pocket as he was leaving, and I'm not ashamed to admit I cast a quick eavesdropping spell. What I heard didn't instill much confidence.

A woman picked up and asked if he'd managed to get the job done.

"Not yet," he said. "I don't think she'd do it, no matter what we offered her. I think we may have misread her and her brother has more influence than we'd thought."

"That's not your decision," the woman answered. "Just do what we sent you there to do." She disconnected, and my heart sank.

I ended the spell and closed my ward behind him.

"That didn't sound good," Tempe said as I closed the door and twisted the deadbolt. Not everybody had magic, and locks were just as effective against them as my wards were; maybe more.

"No, it didn't." I sighed and dropped onto the couch, wondering how he'd made it past my bullshit meter so completely.

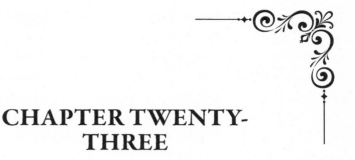

CHAPTER TWENTY-THREE

I'D TOSSED AND TURNED most of the night, so when I dragged myself into the bathroom to get ready for work the next morning, I looked like death warmed over. I didn't feel much better.

I jumped into the shower and used some of Mila's mood-boosting shampoo. It smelled heavenly and did the trick. By the time I stepped out of the shower, I felt good and was ready to face the day.

As usual, people were already in the pool and on the beach when I got there. Bob was off, so I was serving and Dimitri was bartending for the day. That was kind of a good thing because I could use the upbeat energy he brought. He was already slicing fruit, and the Bloody Mary mix was out.

I raised a brow. "Hair of the dog, or is somebody just starting early?"

"Hair of the dog, I think. Lila's out there and has more bags under her eyes than you do."

Scowling, I touched my face. "I don't have bags under my eyes." I should know because that was yet another concoction Mila'd given me, and it had worked like a charm. Probably because it was one.

"You have some smudges," he said.

"Smudges aren't bags."

"They're baby bags," he said, handing me a couple slices of cucumber. "Here, put these on."

I tossed them back at him, along with a suggestion for what he could do with the ones he hadn't already sliced and put in the water cooler. That was another of his concoctions—cucumber-lime water. It wasn't horrible and a lot of people loved it, but I thought it was weird. As far as I was concerned, cucumbers were just pickles that hadn't been made yet.

After I took care of the paperwork from the day before, I went out to check on the guests. In addition to being acting manager, I was also waitressing. Blake needed to find somebody soon because I wasn't interested in advancing my career.

My first stop was at the pool. It was designed in a T-shape, with a lounging ledge that went all the way around the deep end. One side of the T had a canopy drawn over it, which made it nice for anybody who wanted to be in the water but couldn't or didn't want to be in the sun.

I set my tray on the table and stepped down onto the lounging ledge beside Lila, enjoying the feel of cool water on my feet.

"What's up, chica," I asked.

She took a sip from her Bloody Mary, but her heart wasn't in it.

"I'm about to give up on the whole man thing," she said.

Lila was an undine, which was a water nymph rumored to need a man to obtain a soul and achieve immortality. That was just an old wives' tale perpetuated by undine mamas looking to keep their daughters out of trouble and get them properly married off.

However, it was also a common misconception that if the man cheated, he died. Well, it wasn't really a misconception so much as the method behind it was wrong. There was no major death woowoo behind it; nymphs just got super pissy when their men cheated, and sometimes it got out of hand.

I was pretty sure Southern gals and undines played significant roles in starting the whole *wrath of a woman scorned* thing. However, it did tend to scare off potential suitors.

Stephanie, the Valkyrie I'd talked to the day Cass bit the big one, was sunbathing on a lounger a few feet over, just barely out of the shade. She put her hand over her eyes like a visor to block the sun. "What do you need a man for, anyway? I've never seen the draw."

Speaking of wrath of a woman scorned. Except a Valkyrie didn't really need to be scorned to rain down some wrath. It was just what they did.

"You know," Lila said, blushing.

"Oh," Stephanie said with a snort. "Just pick one up that appeals to you, then. You don't need to keep him."

"But I want one to love, and to love me back," the nymph said, stirring her drink.

"Then I don't know what to tell you," Stephanie said. "Long-term relationships really aren't my thing." She put her head back on the lounger and closed her eyes, withdrawing from the conversation.

I pulled in a deep breath and released it. What was it about love recently? First Stan, now Lila. Different points of view, true, but *affairs of the heart* issues seemed to be the problem of the week.

"Look," I said. "The right guy will come along."

I offered up some of the options I'd given to Stan. She could transform into a humanesque form with legs and could even choose to live on land if she wanted.

Thinking back to Blake and the conversation I'd overheard Colin having the night before, I was kinda leaning in the same direction as Steph was, at least for the moment.

I pushed to my feet because frankly, the conversation was depressing me.

I'd no sooner made it back to the bar than the alarm on my phone went off. Speaking of cheating men, it was time to go meet with Blake about the whole Lucy thing.

Even though I was wishing for some distraction to blow up that would give me a legitimate excuse to blow him off, it came in a form that made me wish I'd been more specific with my wish.

A bald dwarf dressed like an accountant was waiting at the bar with Dimitri and pushed off the stool when I approached. He was several inches shorter than I was and looked like he'd smelled something dead.

"Destiny Maganti?" he asked.

I narrowed my eyes, unwilling to fess up to who I was to a stranger, given the events of the last few days. "Who's asking?"

"Dwight Nightingale, PCIB. I assume you *are* Ms. Maganti?" He flipped out his creds, and I examined them; they were real.

I huffed out a breath. "Yeah, I'm Destiny Maganti."

"Then you're under arrest for the murder of Cassiel, former Angel of Temperance. Please come with me."

A familiar voice sounded behind me, and my knees went weak with relief. "I'm Colin Moore, Ms. Maganti's attorney. From here on out, she'll be speaking through me, and I'll need to see what evidence you have against her."

Mr. Nightingale curled his lip. "I'm afraid I'm not at liberty to discuss that."

"And I'm afraid I'm going to have to insist," Colin replied, stepping in front of me. For once in my life, I was happy to zip it and let somebody else do the talking, because I was afraid I was going to throw up.

"Very well, then," Mr. Short and Snippy said. "We found traces of death essence in her home."

CHAPTER TWENTY-FOUR

I PLOPPED BACKWARDS, and for once, something went my way. Dimitri was fast enough to see me toppling and made it over the bar in time to scoot a stool under me.

"What do you mean you found traces of death essence in my house? That's not possible," I said.

"Actually, it was in several different places," he said. "We found traces in your bathroom as well as on a dirty apron in your laundry basket."

"That's easy enough to explain," Colin said. "She cleaned up the mess after they took Cassiel away. She must have gotten it on her at that point."

"Or it could have leaked out of the vial into the pocket of the apron," he said. "It's up to the tribunal to decide. Until then, I'm going to have to insist that she come with me."

Colin held up one finger. "Before you take her anywhere, I need to make a phone call. Trust me—it would behoove you to allow me the latitude."

Nightingale heaved a disgusted sigh but motioned for him to go ahead. "You have two minutes. I'm a busy man."

Colin pulled his phone out and thumbed through his contacts 'til he found the number he was looking for. Stuffing his finger into his ear, he walked to the other side of the bar out of hearing range.

I longed to know what he was saying and who he was saying it to but didn't want to bite the hand that was feeding me by eavesdropping. Then I noticed Tempe sitting on a stool just a few feet from where he was at, her head tilted, listening.

He returned in less than his allotted time and smirked at the little troll—excuse me, dwarf—as the man's phone rang.

"You'll want to get that," Colin said, crossing his arms and smirking at the agent.

Just as Colin had, Nightingale turned away from us to answer his phone. He came back less than a minute later, and if looks could kill, Colin and I would both be goners.

"It seems you've been granted special treatment, Ms. Maganti. You're under house arrest until your trial; you're not to leave the resort."

He waved his hand, and a golden band appeared around my ankle.

I knew I shouldn't, but I couldn't help myself. I held out my ankle, examining the new piece of jewelry. "Do you have this in silver? Yellow gold really isn't my thing."

"No silver," Colin said. "Werewolf, remember?"

"Oh yeah," I said, turning back to the agent. "White gold or titanium, then?"

"Jest now, Ms. Maganti. The penalty for your crime is death." With that, he snapped his fingers and disappeared.

"You probably shouldn't have goaded him," Colin said.

I waved him off. I was more interested in learning who my benefactor was.

"So, who'd you call?"

"I'm not at liberty to say, but I'll be sure to pass on your gratitude," he replied.

Tempe's voice sounded in my head.

He didn't say any names. All he did was give them a brief rundown of the situation, and the woman on the other end said she'd take care of it.

Great. Even with an eavesdropping fox, I was still as clueless as I had been five minutes ago.

I pulled my phone out of my pocket and called Michael. He didn't pick up, so I left a voicemail asking him to call me back. I also sent an 811 text. That was our code for, "Death isn't imminent, but I *am* in a world of shit."

My next call was to Blake.

"Where are you?" he snapped. "You were supposed to be here ten minutes ago."

"Yeah," I said. "About that. As much as I wanted to discuss your love life, I was in the process of being arrested for killing Cass."

"Discuss my ... wait, what?"

"Yeah, a Dwight Nightingale showed up to arrest me, but Colin somehow managed to get me house arrest instead. It seems when I cleaned up the mess after they took Cass away, I got some of the death essence on my apron."

He was silent for a minute. "They're supposed to go through me whenever there's any kind of issue at the resort."

"I just told you that I've been arrested for a crime punishable by death, and your takeaway is they left you out of the process?" It's a good thing I was talking to him on the phone rather than in person, because he would have been in danger of being turned into a mosquito.

"It has nothing to do with ego, Destiny, and everything to do with proper representation. As an employee of the resort, you have access to a number of legal resources."

As usual, Colin was within hearing distance and eavesdropping. I'd get onto him, except in my experience, it was almost impossible to shame a werewolf. He pasted a bored expression on his face and twirled a finger in the air, making the *big whoop* gesture.

I thought about his connections to the angel world and couldn't decide if I was in good hands with him or not.

Margo's words drifted back through my head. *When you have to make a choice, have faith.*

I took a deep breath, closed my eyes, and stepped off the ledge, hoping this was the situation she was referring to. "That's okay. Colin's got everything under control."

My new attorney and possible friend-maybe-more grinned and gave me a thumbs-up.

Margo, you better be right.

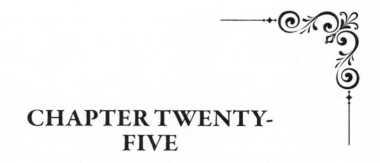

CHAPTER TWENTY-FIVE

BLAKE OFFERED TO GIVE me the rest of the day off, but I figured working might help keep my mind off the possibility that I may be dead within a week. That's really not something I wanted to dwell on.

They'd set my tribunal hearing for exactly a week. Trials in the magical world followed the *right to a speedy* trial credo much better than in the human world, possibly because the process was streamlined with magic. Plus, on the whole, magical folks tended to commit fewer crimes for two reasons.

First, punishments on our side of things were no joke. They weren't intended to rehabilitate the criminal, so there was no mollycoddling. If you stole something, there was a real possibility you could lose a finger for the second offense. First offenses, if they were minor, were often given special consideration depending on the circumstances, but repeat offenders didn't get off with just a slap on the wrist, unless it was with a cat-o-nine.

Next, if you committed a crime and were busted by the human police, you ran the risk of outing the magical world, or at the very least finding yourself unable to use your powers while you were locked up. Magical punishment for doing so was uber bad.

You know those cases of when people just die in their cells but there's no apparent cause? There's a cause.

Anyway, all of that was exactly what I was trying to avoid thinking about, so I trotted down to the water bar to check on a group of merfolks and sirens Dax and Amber had brought to celebrate a two-hundredth wedding anniversary. Those were always fun because there were no fines for drunk driving and they couldn't drown. Since they were strictly off-limits to sharks and other predators, there was no real reason for them to hold back.

The only downside was that it wasn't unusual to be tipped in treasure rather than cash. Sometimes it was an old spoon that had a fancy design—merpeople were attracted to shiny things, and if they weren't familiar with land-dwelling currency, what was extremely valuable to them would end up a re-gift to another water dweller later.

However, there are many shiny things that *do* have value in the sea. I received three gold coins once that, thanks to time and wear, were just discs of gold. Those netted me a couple killer pairs of boots and were a nice addition to my nest egg, too.

"Hey, Des!" Dax called. "Any updates? We haven't been up to the pool yet."

"Meh," I said, unwilling to rain on their parade. "It's not going as well as I'd hoped, but I have faith things will shake out the way they're supposed to."

"Atta girl," Amber said. "No need to borrow trouble. You're a good egg. They'll do the right thing." She gave me a conspiratorial glance and waggled her eyebrows. "Not that we were being nosy or anything, but we couldn't help but notice that a certain werewolf couldn't take his eyes off of you yesterday."

"Yeah," Roxi, the one celebrating her bicentennial anniversary, said, "and rumor has it, there was almost some lip-locking going on after you pulled your boards out of the water."

I shook my head. The worst thing about the resort is that just because you thought you were alone didn't mean you were.

Elves and faeries would wander in the custom-built rain forests to commune, and water folks lived for a good love story. Or any story for that matter. They were a gossipy bunch and had a better information dissemination tree than my grandmother's beauty salon did. That was saying something.

Smiling slyly, Dax said, "Ooh, is there finally another love interest we need to know about?"

The sirens were smiling, too, though they were a little scary because of all the sharp, pointy teeth.

Sylvia, one of the youngest in the group, gave me a toothy grin. "You'll have to bring him swimming so we can get a close-up."

Even though I knew the girls were harmless—at least to me—a little shiver still ran down my spine just thinking about them swimming underneath me. Of course, they were better than dolphins when it came to keeping sharks at bay, so at least I had that thought to comfort me.

I smiled back. "I'll be sure to do that. Though we're just getting to know each other. There's no love in the air just yet."

I shook my head. There it was again, and it wasn't even spring. Of course, we did live in the land of eternal paradise, so I guess that contributed to the warm-and-fuzzies, especially when you threw in a couple of Bob's margaritas or Dimitri's Mai Tais.

I don't know what he added to those, but I suspected it was a faerie thing rather than just supplies that were readily available behind the bar. Speaking of, that's what Steph was drinking, and she was probably ready for another.

There were a few empty cups that had blown out of the trash, and I couldn't help but think about the crappy exchange I'd had with Cass the morning he'd died. He was an ass, but as much as I'd disliked him, I hadn't meant it when I'd wished him dead.

Off the coast and away from me forever? Absolutely. But not dead. I wondered what had happened to his soul. I mean, nobody really knows what happens when you die. Even folks who come back as ghosts don't get a glimpse of the other side. Some report seeing a bright light, while some just say they woke up dead.

We had a crew of ghosts that lived in Georgia who liked to come to the resort to vacation. We had a post-living bartender named Jeff we called in when they were on-property. I wasn't exactly sure how it worked, because ghosts typically couldn't eat or drink, but he'd keeled over in his own bar and somehow managed to bring his booze and mixers with him to the other side.

Needless to say, he was a huge draw once word made it through the living-impaired community. Blake had been searching for a chef that had died under similar circumstances. If he could find one, we'd have the whole ghostly resort market locked down. We wouldn't make money off them, but they'd bring their living friends and family, who had real cash to spend.

Anyway, the point is that none of them knew how they'd ended up ghosts or what was on the other side.

Wherever Cass was, I hoped he was happier there than he had been with us.

CHAPTER TWENTY-SIX

SCOOPING UP THE CUPS that had brought on the ghostly rabbit trail, I shoved them into the trash and headed to the pool to check on Steph and Lila. Both were ready for a refill, and Lila's mood had improved considerably.

Thank goodness she was a happy drunk. I'd had a group of harpies in a few weeks before, on vacation after the death of a loved one. Lemme tell you—those gals gave new meaning to the term *ugly crying*. It wasn't a situation I was eager to repeat anytime soon.

A vampire family had joined the mix and asked me about renting a cabana. Even though the resort was spelled to allow them to enjoy the sunshine, they were prone to sunburn just because they were so white. I took their drink orders and told them to take their pick of cabanas. They were the first people of the day to ask for one.

I slapped my tray up on the bar and gave Dimitri my order. While I was waiting, my phone rang; it was Michael.

"Des, I just heard they sent Nightingale after you. Where are you? I assume since you answered your phone that Blake has a resort rep dealing with them? Nightingale's a jerk with Napoleon Syndrome, though—"

"Michael!" I barked, stopping his doom-and-gloom chattering. "Colin was here when Nightingale tried to arrest me. He made a single phone call, and all of a sudden I was placed under house arrest rather than being hauled off to jail."

"Who did he call?" Suspicion laced his tone, just as it had mine when I'd asked.

"I don't know. He wouldn't say, and even though Tempest overheard the conversation, he didn't say anything other than I was being arrested and why. Less than a minute later, the agent's phone rang and I was wearing a golden anklet."

"Speaking of that, *do not* leave the boundaries. It would be ... unpleasant," he said.

"Yeah, I kinda figured that when they made me sign that my relatives would be responsible for replacement of the device if I were to breach the terms of the house arrest."

"So what do they have on you that made them arrest you?" he asked.

"I must have gotten death essence on my apron when I was cleaning up the mess," I said. "I guess they found it when they searched my house yesterday."

"That's not good," he said. "Good thing for the resort, it's only toxic to angels. If they'd followed protocol, a hazmat team would have come in to clean it up."

"Nobody wishes that would have been the way it went down more than I do," I said, my tone wry as I placed the drinks Dimitri'd lined up in front of me on the tray. "But woulda, coulda, shoulda."

My neck was cramping from holding my phone between my ear and shoulder. "Listen, Michael, I'm working and need to go. Is there anything else I should be doing?"

"As bad as I hate to say it, do what Colin says. If he took you on, he did it for a reason."

"Okay," I said. "Keep in touch if you find anything out."

I disconnected and scooped up the drink tray, already way beyond over the whole situation. I hated feeling helpless, but this was way outside my wheelhouse. For better or worse, I was gonna have to do exactly what Michael said—trust Colin to have my back. I just prayed he didn't do it to make me a sitting duck rather than a free bird.

After settling the vampires into their cabana and putting in their lunch orders, I decided to join Steph and Lila back by the pool. Steph was regaling her with the details of one of her recent battles with great flourish, her face flushed with memories of glorious beheadings and perfect, mid-air heart shots.

Lila, on the other hand, was trying to smile and be supportive, but she was a little green around the gills.

I smiled and brought them a cracker tray, figuring if it worked for nauseated pregnant women and people with the flu, it might help somebody with vivid descriptions of death and destruction floating through her head. She gave me a wobbly smile and nibbled on one, her Bloody Mary forgotten in favor of the Sprite I'd brought.

Steph was amazing, but I was glad she usually came alone. The last time she'd brought friends, the place had turned from peaceful seaside resort to something that resembled a Civil War reenactment zone, except the war whoops were louder. I'd had to put a sound-dampening spell around the pool area because people were complaining and canceling food orders.

We'd just made it through the lunch rush when Michael called again.

"Hey, that was quick," I said when I answered.

"Well, I figure we don't have much time. I have to solve an angel murder in less time that it usually takes me to catch somebody selling war charms or military-grade armor."

That sounded like something that would take months, and the fact that he was implying it only took a week for him to catch somebody doing that made me rethink talking to the strange but nice guy in line behind me at the coffee shop.

"So what did you learn? Have you figured out who Colin talked to? Because if so, I owe them a huge thanks." I crinkled my brow, thinking about other reasons somebody may have for keeping me locked to the resort. "Or at least I think I do."

"No," he said. "No luck there yet, but I have even better news. I've managed to track down the gargoyles Cass hung out with. And boy, do they have a story to tell."

Steph waved me over, and I cringed when I saw why. Poor Lila was experiencing round two of her Bloody Marys—and not in a good way. I held up a finger, then went to grab a wet towel and some ice. People didn't realize that heat accelerated the effects of alcohol, especially for folks who weren't used to drinking.

"So don't keep me waiting!" I said, getting irritated from the combination of his procrastination and Lila's heaving. When it came to somebody being sick, I took myself out of the equation as soon as I got them out of any area I was responsible for cleaning up.

Steph gave me an apologetic smile when I handed her the cool rag and bucket of ice. I winked at her in thanks as I turned back around and took my phone from between my cheek and shoulder. I hated being on the phone while I was dealing directly with a guest, but not nearly as bad as I hated the idea of dying a painful death before the week was out.

"Okay, here's the thing," Michael said. "The gargoyle said he got the death essence—we're still trying to get him to tell us from where—for Cass. But when he went to hand it to him under the table, it was gone from his pocket. Apparently, Cass was going to take out another angel in order to get back into the flock, and he was pissed."

"That's really the name for a group of angels?" I asked.

"Focus, Des," he said, exasperated. "Whatever they call themselves, he thought he'd figured out a way to get back in, and that meant killing another angel."

"That sounds like a horrible plan," I said, then remembered who I was talking about.

"It was, but at least we know now who brought the essence, who wanted it, what it was going to be used for, and that it disappeared sometime between when they got to the tiki and when he reached into his pocket at the table."

"Yeah," I said with a big sigh. "Now we just need to figure out how it ended up in Cass's drink."

"Yeah, I haven't really worked my way around to that part yet," he said.

"I'd appreciate it if you would," I replied. "I don't have time to be executed next week. I have a nail appointment."

"You know, lots of women have their nails done post-mortem, so you really don't need to cancel the appointment," he said.

"Thanks for the confidence boost, bro."

"Anytime, little sister. And Des?"

"Yeah?"

"I love you, and I'm doing everything I can, okay?"

My throat tightened. "Okay," I croaked. Considering the source, those two phrases together both terrified me and comforted me at the same time. "I love you, too."

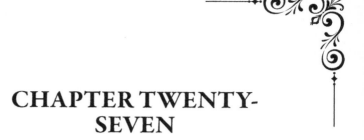

CHAPTER TWENTY-SEVEN

I FIGURED I'D BETTER call Colin and bring him up to speed. I was glad when he picked up after a couple rings, because after the exchange with Michael, I felt the noose tightening and hoped the feeling stayed proverbial rather than literal.

"I'll call you right back," he said after I explained what Michael had learned, then hung up before I could say anything else. What was it with people just hitting the *end* button without so much as a bye?

The vampire family's food was up, and I did something I never did—I snapped my fingers and magicked it down to them, along with fresh drinks. I'd go check on them in a couple minutes, but I needed time to process the new info first.

Dimitri was standing directly across the bar from me, gazing at me with sympathy. "I can't believe they're trying to put this off on you," he said. "Of all the people on this resort that I'd peg as a murderer, you'd be last on the list."

"Yeah," I sighed. "I need to learn to keep my mouth shut. If I hadn't wished him dead, this wouldn't be happening."

"You don't know that," he said, reaching across to pat my hand. "Tell me what's going on, and I'll help you think. I can tell from the look on your face you're trying to puzzle it out, so two heads are better than one." He gave his head a shake. "Especially when one of them has hair this fabulous."

I smiled at his attempt to cheer me up, then relayed the story for the second time. My brain still wasn't collating the info, and I felt like there were still huge chunks of the puzzle missing.

"Well, that's easy, then," he said, looking at me as if I were five and having problems with a math problem.

I raised a brow. "Really, then. Please, do tell."

"It was the hookers. Or at least one of them. It couldn't have been anybody else."

Thinking back, he had a point. All three of them had been sitting in a lap, and I'd sort of felt the need to call for a hand check, though I was afraid of what they might have pulled up along with their hands if I did.

"You're right," I said. "It would have been cake for one of them to pick the gargoyle's pocket. I don't know how easy it would have been for her to get it into his drink, though."

Dimitri reached below the bar, and in less than a blink of an eye, there was a wedge of lime on the bar in front of me. He'd been so fast that, to my eye, it hadn't been there one second but was the next. I barely saw his hand move.

"Don't forget, sweetie. The hand is often faster than the eye."

I glanced down again, and the lime was gone.

"I wish I'd been here that day," he said. "I've worked in some shady places in my time, and maybe I'd recognize them."

I perked up. "I have video actually, or I can get one in a heartbeat."

Pulling my phone from my pocket, I texted Michael and asked him to send me the security video Blake had sent him the day we'd been in Abbadon's Gate.

While we waited, he poured me a lime water and I took a gulp of it.

My phone dinged with an incoming text less than a minute later. I pulled up the video and handed him my phone.

He squinted at it, trying to make out the faces.

"I know these three," he said, "but there's a problem."

He turned the phone so I could see it and pointed at the one sitting on Cass's lap. "This one here, Ronni, married a vampire. He just turned her like a month ago. I know because she was actually a sweetheart who life had kicked around. I was happy for her when she met her husband and left the life, pardon the pun."

My mind flashed back to the second the girl's glamour had slipped. I'd thought she was just trying to make herself look better, but she'd made herself look like somebody else altogether.

"She wore a glamour," I said.

"Did you get a look at her underneath?" he asked, sliding a coaster under my water.

"Not really," I said. "It only slipped for a second. I saw brunette hair, but that's it."

"Then it seems we're one step closer to figuring it out, except there are about a hundred different species that can pull off a glamour."

"Yeah, but we have to figure it was at least humanoid, because he was actually touching her. She had to feel right, or he would have picked up on it."

He sighed. "It probably helped her cause that he was likely either already drinking or still half-drunk from the night before."

"A little bit of both, as usual," I said.

I picked up my tray and went to check on Steph and Lila. Dax and crew had moved from the water bar to the pool and asked for another round. I'd no sooner delivered them than Colin waved to me from the end of the bar. Once he had my attention, he motioned me over to a table.

Somebody else was sitting there, her face covered by her hair, tapping away on her phone.

When she looked up, I didn't know whether to run or sling a spell at her.

The woman who'd been following me in Abaddon's Gate looked up at me and smiled.

Colin put his hand on the small of my back, and I didn't know whether he was doing it to reassure me or to keep me from bolting. Either way, I was grateful for it, even though the moment felt surreal.

"Destiny Maganti, I'd like you to meet Eva, assistant to Arariel, Angel of Water, and founding member of the Enchanted Coast."

CHAPTER TWENTY-EIGHT

I LOOKED BACK AND FORTH between them. "You gotta be kidding me."

"I assure you we're not," Eva said. "I'm sorry we got off to a rocky start, but I was just supposed to follow you." Her face flushed with embarrassment, and she gave me a pained smile. "It seems I'm not cut out for subterfuge."

"No," I said, putting my tray on the bar and sliding into a chair across from her. "You should probably stick to ... whatever else it is an angel's assistant does."

"I agree," she said.

"Listen, I'm not sure why you're here, but before we go any further, I need to tell Colin something."

I explained the whole Ronni situation and was surprised when Eva narrowed her eyes and steepled her fingers in front of her.

"You say the person behind the glamour was a brunette?"

"Yeah," I said, "but that's really all I can tell you about her. It was only a second, more like a double-exposure blur than an actual glimpse."

"That's okay," she said, tapping out something else on her phone. "That's helped tremendously."

"So do you mind if I ask why you were following me to begin with?" I asked. "I mean, if Ari wanted to talk to me, why didn't he just come here?"

"I'm not at liberty to discuss exactly what he's doing, but he's got his hands full with a mess in DC right now, and before that, one of his brothers was throwing a temper tantrum about the movie industry and had decided to crash a tidal wave onto the shores of LA. I swear, the Angel of Water was not created to put out fires, but it seems that's been his role lately."

She sighed. "Which leaves me to fill roles I'm not suited to, even though I've been given additional clearance."

"Okay," I said, feeling her pain on a much smaller scale, since I was looking at a yawning future of managing the tiki while also working at it. Tourist season was going to be insane if Blake didn't find somebody between now and then. "But I still don't know what that has to do with me."

"Well," she said, clearing her throat, "I definitely don't have the security clearance to go there." I scowled at her, and she held out her hands, brows raised. "But I promise it's not anything bad. It's just ... Ari wants to present the idea to you himself."

I pulled in a deep breath, then released it. "Then what, exactly, is it that you *can* tell me?"

She brightened, and I was guessing she was relieved I'd dropped it. Rather than continue, though, she motioned to Colin and nodded.

"They were considering bringing Cass back in. This was never meant to be a permanent exile, and some felt it had gone on long enough. Believe it or not, Cass wasn't always bitter. He had quite a few friends up there," he said. "But there was a certain faction that was all for leaving him here to rot. They considered him an embarrassment to their kind. One angel in particular was adamant. The rest were on the fence, but she'd whipped them into a frenzy of righteous indignation."

I raised my brow at the term.

"Well, that's what it was," he said. "In the most literal form possible. But my guess is that Cass figured if he took her out, they'd scatter and he'd be back in."

I thought it over and bounced my head left and right. "To be fair, you can't really blame them. The guy was a drunken tool."

A small smile flitted across Eva's face.

"And that's what you were talking to him about?" I asked. "Why you were here to begin with?"

Dimitri brought us over a pitcher of water and three glasses, and I poured us all one just to give my hands something to do.

"Yeah," Colin said. "I had two options for him that had been decided on by the majority. If he was willing to stop drinking, he could have his old position back. If not, Di—the angel dead set against his return—insisted he be stripped of his wings and left here, mortal."

I whistled. "Wow. That was some decision he had to make."

I remembered Bob mentioning the threat he'd heard Colin throw at Cass. "So that's what you meant when you said he was making you do something you didn't want to do?"

Colin nodded, picking at his coaster. "Yeah. I mean, I didn't like the guy. But I didn't want to do that to him, either. And it would have been so easy for him. Angels aren't susceptible to human addictions—or at least not drugs and alcohol—so it's not like he *couldn't* quit drinking. He just wasn't willing to."

"And this chick who was all for knocking him clear off the ladder once and for all—you think that's who he'd planned to kill?"

"Yeah, though how he was planning to do it is beyond me."

"Oh," Eva answered, "I can explain that. She was coming here to vacation with Ari next week."

Wow, so she'd have died just like he did. Justice, in a roundabout way.

"That's who you think killed him, then?"

She gave a little shrug. "I guess we'll never know now, will we? You can bet there will be an investigation, but angels play by much different rules than we do."

My mind was whirring, trying to think of questions that would tie up all the loose ends. Tempe jumped into my lap.

"Who was the man in front of the chocolate shop?" she asked. "And why were you rushing toward us like that?"

Her black eye was still visible around the edges of her aviators, and I felt a twinge of guilt. I reminded myself she'd been following me, then rushed toward me like I was under attack.

Speaking of, another question popped to the front of my head.

"Who lured me there? Who was the fake Michael?"

"Yeah," she said, cringing, "I'm afraid that's another piece of information that's above my pay grade. To be honest, I only have speculation and personal suspicions about that at this point anyway. I mean, I know who he was but not why he was there, for sure. I suspect he was hired by the gargoyles because you'd gotten too close to finding the truth."

I scrubbed my hand over my face. "No offense, but for somebody here to give me information, you're not telling me much."

"I know, and I'm sorry. But you'll have all the answers soon, I promise." She cast an unsure glance at Colin, who just shrugged.

"Maybe," she added, and I rolled my eyes.

"Well then," I said, pushing up from the table. "Now that everything is clear as mud, I have guests to attend to."

Angels, I thought as I walked away. That's what happened when you gave a bunch of spoiled brats power over the earth. I was glad I'd never have that much power.

But never say never, as I was to learn much, much later.

CHAPTER TWENTY-NINE

WITH ALL OF THE ANGEL stuff settled, Dwight Nightingale had to eat a little crow and unfetter me. I thought he was going to have a stroke when I offered him a lollipop once I was loose. Some people just had no sense of humor.

At least I knew who the fake Michael was, but they wouldn't tell me why Eva'd been following me. They did say it was for my own safety.

Stupid angels. But when I learned she was watching out for me, I felt uber bad about giving her the black eye.

Blake insisted I take the day off, and now that I knew what Colin had been hiding, I was okay with him.

"I'm sorry I couldn't tell you," he said as we walked along the beach.

"Nah, it's okay," I bent down to pick up a shell. "I get it. I mean, I have famous people—or infamous ones—who come in here, and I maintain their privacy. Samuel L Jackson could be staying here, and as much as I'd fangirl, I'd do it in private. You'd never know."

He cut his eyes sideways at me. "Is he here?"

I widened my eyes. It had long been a suspicion that nobody could be that badass without being magical, but I'd never met the man. Still, I owed Colin a little payback, and I pasted my best sorry-not sorry face on and waved a dismissive hand.

"Client-cabana girl confidentiality. I'm not at liberty to discuss our private guests."

"I'm here for as long as I want to be, you know. If he's here, I'll see him."

Raising a brow, I rubbed my chin and narrowed my eyes in speculation. "Will you, though?"

He gave me a little shove sideways.

"Let's go back to the tiki," I said. "I'm starving."

"Not yet." He bent down and picked up a smooth, flat piece of stone that had probably been part of a ship at some point centuries ago. Rubbing it between his fingers, he turned to the smooth-as-glass surface of the water and skipped it across.

"Ow!" a voice cried from several yards out. I let my eyes roam the water until I saw Sylvia treading water and rubbing her forehead. "Why'd you do that?"

"Sorry!" Colin called. "I didn't see you there."

"Yeah, okay," she called back before she sank back beneath the surface. "But watch it from now on. You coulda put my eye out."

He glanced at me, and I just shrugged. "Welcome to my world. Now," I said, "I'm tired of walking and I'm starving. I haven't eaten today because I've been too shaken up worrying about dying and stuff."

I turned back in the direction of the tiki, and he took my hand. We walked in silence for a while, just enjoying the ocean breeze and the sound of the ocean. We were almost back to the tiki before I noticed about a kazillion balloons were waving in the breeze from all around the place.

I scrunched my brow in confusion. "What's going on?"

He gave me a know-it-all smile. "You'll see."

The wind shifted once we were past the water bar, and the smell of burgers made my stomach growl. Colin kept his eyes straight ahead, so I started moving faster. I planned to use every ounce of my considerable charm to con a burger and a dog out of whoever was partying.

I stepped up onto the pool deck. A huge banner with *Congratulations* scrawled across it in giant, colorful letters floated in the air at the end of the pool, and smoke billowed from the big barbecue grill we kept there for special occasions and private parties.

Looking around, I realized I knew everybody there. Some were folks I worked with—Bob and Jolene and the kids, Dimitri, Elena—and others were regulars. Elsa and Tolthe, Cyri, Steph, Lila (who was looking less green), the selkies, and even Arariel and Eva. I narrowed my eyes because he was supposedly in LA.

"What's going on?" I asked Colin.

"Ask Blake," he said.

I glanced over, and sure enough, there was Blake. He looked down at my hand, which was still interlocked with Colin's, and a little flicker of sadness shadowed his eyes for a second.

Lucy was standing beside him, except she was holding hands with a linebacker-looking guy, who was smiling at me, too. I didn't have time to contemplate that, though.

With flair, Blake turned toward the congrats sign and poofed his hands. Two more smaller banners unrolled beneath it. One said *Employee of the Year*, and the other had my name on it.

Blake and Lucy stepped toward me, and Tempe jumped into my arms.

"Destiny Maganti, I'd like you to meet Lucy Flanders, president of the Enchanted Coast Board of Directors, and her husband, Stephen. Lucy, Stephen—Destiny."

They led me forward toward the banner, where there was a huge cake with *Congratulations, Destiny* sprawled across it.

Blake leaned down. "Red velvet on one half, marble on the other. Your two favorites."

I smiled at him and realized I still loved him, but I didn't know if I could ever forgive him.

Ari stepped forward and produced a large envelope out of thin air, then stood beside me. "I asked if I could do the honors, since, you know, I witnessed your exemplary serving skills when you almost dumped an entire tray of drinks on the Angel of War's wife."

I grinned at him. "I always say, if you're gonna do it, do it big!"

He squeezed my shoulder and pulled a microphone out of thin air. "Destiny Maganti, it's my honor to name you Enchanted Coast Employee of the Year. Your dedication, positive attitude, and spirit of teamwork combine to make you an employee others respect and admire. Thank you for doing your best to provide only the highest level of service to each and every guest who passes through here."

He handed me the envelope, and I tucked it under my arm.

"Open it, you little dope," he said out of the corner of his mouth, his eyes sparkling.

I did, and there was the plaque as I suspected, and I held it up to show to the crowd, who cheered me on. There were two smaller envelopes in there, too, so I pulled them out. One had a considerable bonus check, and the other held an invitation for me and a plus-one to the Angel's Ball, an annual event that was the paranormal equivalent of the Oscars.

He grinned and hugged me. "Seriously, Des, thank you," he said in my ear.

"It's my pleasure, Ari, truly. Though I understand you want to talk to me about something."

"Now's not the time, but it's coming," he said. "Patience."

Angels!

I stood looking out over my friends and glanced to my right at the two men who represented my past and maybe my future.

There was a fat check in my envelope, burgers on the grill, people I cared about surrounded me, and everybody was happy.

That, to me, was one of those perfect moments in time. As the sea breeze whispered across my neck and happiness filled the air, I realized my life was truly enchanted, and there was nowhere else on earth I'd rather be.

Thank You!

I know my style isn't for everybody. Know that I appreciate your time and kind words via email and reviews. Thanks for giving me a few hours of your time and I hope you enjoyed meeting Destiny and spending time on the Enchanted Coast. If you'd please take a minute to leave a review so others can decide whether this series is for them, I would be grateful.

Hopefully, we'll meet up again in Book 2, The Surfboard Slaying[1]. 'Til then, happy reading!

If you'd like to read the first chapter, keep reading. ☺

The Surfboard Slaying

Chapter 1 Sneak Peek

"EXCUSE ME, BUT MAY I use your sunscreen? I hate to be a mooch, but I seem to have gone through mine already."

I pulled the towel off my eyes and leaned up onto my elbow on my poolside lounge chair, squinting as my eyes adjusted to the sun. A twenty-something woman with light skin and dark hair rested on her elbow facing me from the next chair over, her over-sized sunglasses pulled up just enough that her chocolate-colored eyes were visible beneath them as she waited for my answer. She had a soft southern lilt to her voice. I tilted my head. Alabama, or Mississippi maybe.

I'd heard the scrape of chair legs against the pavers when she'd claimed the chair half an hour ago, but hadn't bothered to look up. It was one of my few days off, and I was enjoying it poolside, soaking up rays in the adults-only infinity pool on the rooftop of the Enchanted Coast Resort where I worked and lived.

I dealt with people enough when I was working that I enjoyed my solitude when I wasn't. The one exception to that was my familiar, a marble fox named Tempest. She hated both water and heat, so she'd opted to hang out at the cottage, napping, rather than hang with me at the pool.

It only took one glance to realize the girl was a vampire, and likely a newly turned one at that based on the pink tinging her skin. The resort was charmed so that even vampires could enjoy the sun and amenities without burning—or wanting to drain other guests dry. Older vampires could endure the sun almost as well as I, a regular Irish witch, could. Newer ones didn't have quite that much tolerance even with the magic.

"Sure," I said, pulling my bottle of SPF 50 from my beach bag and handing it to her.

"Thanks," she said, squeezing a glob out and slathering it over her shoulders and arms. She smeared some on her cheeks and nose too, even though she was wearing an enormous floppy hat. "I've always tanned rather than burned, but have recently acquired a ... health condition that makes me sensitive to UV rays."

I tilted one side of my mouth up in a wry smile at the way she phrased it. "I gathered as much. Go ahead and hang onto it; I have another bottle."

Before I could roll back over and pretend I was alone again, she held out her hand across the space dividing our chairs. "Marissa Clayton."

So much for solitude, but manners prevailed over preference and I reached out and shook her sunscreen-slick hand. "Destiny Maganti. Pleased to meet you."

She leaned back in her chair and I did the same. A comfortable silence ensued for a few minutes.

"So, how long are you here for?" she asked.

I gave a mental groan. Don't get me wrong—I'm a people person, but I'd just come off a stretch of working twelve ten-hour days and just wanted to chill and detune.

"A little over three years," I said without taking the towel off my eyes.

"Three years?" The confusion in her voice made me smile, and I relented.

"Yeah. But to be fair, I work here. And now that I think about it, it's almost four years."

She laughed. "That makes more sense. I'm here for a month to get away from my life. I've got some tough decisions to make, and I'm not sure where I'm going to go from here." She gave a deep sigh and though I didn't want to pry, I felt like she was waiting for me to ask. So I did.

"Sounds like a lot of weight you're carrying. Major life change?"

Another sigh. "You could say that." She paused. "You're magical, right? I mean, everybody here has to be, according to the brochure."

That was another sign she was a noob. Most of us had a sort of second sense about other folks with magic, but newly turned vampires and shifters took a while to develop that even with their heightened sense of smell. To be fair, though, witches are tough to pick from a crowd outside of a place like the resort because we smelled almost like humans. Fortunately, we smelled just different enough to *not* smell tasty to vampires and carnivorous shifters.

"I am," I said, sitting up to see her. "I'm a water witch."

A look of understanding crossed Marissa's face and she smiled. "I should have guessed that from your smell." The pink tinge to her cheeks from the sun darkened just a bit more when she realized how her words sounded. "I'm so sorry. I didn't mean it like that."

I held up a hand and grinned at her discomfort. It was kinda refreshing being around somebody who still had the ability to blush. "It's all good. I know what you mean. And you're a vampire. New to the life, right?"

Chagrin brushed across her face before she managed to hide it.

"Yeah. Though not by choice."

I cocked a brow. Turning a human was taboo except under specific circumstances, and the parent better be able to back up his or her decision to the higher-ups.

She pulled in a deep breath, then released it. Despite the application of fresh sunscreen, her shoulders were turning a darker shade of pink. It wouldn't be much longer before she blistered.

"How bout we move to the shaded end of the pool?" I said, not wanting to see that happen.

One corner of the pool was covered by a large awning to provide shade for this very reason. We gathered our towels and beach bags and relocated to a table where she wouldn't fry to a crisp. The temperature was about ten degrees cooler in the shade, so I wasn't exactly disappointed.

"Now, you were saying you didn't choose to be a vampire. You know there are rules about that, right?"

Marissa nodded. "It wasn't like that, though. I was hit by a pickup when I ran out of a bar after catchin' my lowdown jerk of a boyfriend cozied up in a corner booth with a cocktail waitress."

Okay, that still didn't explain how she'd ended up a vampire unless the truck somehow had venomous fangs in the grill.

"The guy drivin' the truck was a vampire," she said, then her voice turned bitter. "I was stompin' out of the parkin' lot madder'n an old wet hen and not watchin' where I was goin', and poor Ben, one of my late-night regulars, pulled around the curve from the main road and into the parkin' lot. When he hit me, it knocked me backwards into a swampy area and a gator got me by the arm."

I shook my head. That was some serious bad luck.

"Anyway," she continued, pulling a bottle of faux blood from a little cooler she was carrying, "it hit an artery when it bit down, and he got to me just before it dragged me off and finished me. Asked me if I wanted him to save me and told me my life would change forever if he did." She snorted. "I thought he meant somethin' like I'd lose my arm, but I didn't have much choice. The blood was flowin' out of that gash and I was fadin' fast."

Now I saw where it was going. The good Samaritan hadn't done anything wrong, per se. She'd been dying and he'd saved her life.

She popped the straw in the top of the box and took a pull from it.

"He had to shake me back awake twice before I said yes, and the next thing I knew, it was three days later and I was completely healed. He took care of me for the next week, but then I got stubborn and went to work when he ran to the store.

"I worked evening shift at the local 7-Eleven and it took all of ten minutes before I was wanting to suck the life out of the guy I was workin' with—and trust me, the idea of putting *any* part of him in my mouth would have made me gag a week before. So, I went back home before I did anything stupid and sucked it up, pardon the pun."

The blisters on her shoulders were already healed and, feeling the tenderness on my upper legs, I was a little jealous that she wouldn't be itching and peeling in a few days like I would.

"And how long ago was that? Did he take care of you while you adjusted?"

She nodded. "That was two months ago, and he did. I have to give him that. And he felt awful guilty about the whole mess. But the only thing he's guilty of is savin' my life, such that it is." She squared her shoulders. "I'm lucky to be here. But now I have to decide what to do. It's not like once I leave here, I can just run back to the store. For one, it's a crap job, and for another, I don't trust myself yet. That's why Benjamin—the guy who saved me—recommended I come here. No temptation, and it would give me a chance to get away from the whole mess and get some perspective."

"How's that working out for you?" I asked, genuinely curious. It had to be a tough spot to be in.

Marissa gave a small smile, and I was pleased to see that her nose and cheeks were back to their normal, near-white shade. Must be nice to have vampire healing.

"Better than can be expected, actually. Out there, when I was thirsty, people smelled better than fresh-baked bread, bacon, and coffee, all rolled into one. I walked around droolin' all the time, and could barely focus on just walkin' down the street. I don't have that problem here," she said, wrinkling her nose. "No offense."

I smiled. "None taken. So what about the career thing?"

She shrugged. "With eternity ahead of me, lots of things I figured were outta reach seem a lot more doable now. Plus, not that I was dim before, but my brain works faster. I have options."

"And what about Benjamin?" She was young and pretty and seemed super sweet. I couldn't help but wonder if the connection and all that time together had kindled a flame.

She waved me off and made an *oh puhlease* face. "Trust me—it's not like that. He's old-fashioned—as in 1700s old-fashioned. Plus, since he's the one who turned me, he's kinda paternal. He cares about me, though he has no idea what to do with a modern woman in the house. But now that you mention it, I've noticed several handsome men here, one in particular."

I smelled gossip, and hoped the conversation was taking a turn for the juicy. She shut me down before I could ask.

"Enough about me though," Marissa said, turning the conversation. "What's it like working at a place like this? Do you live here, too? And is that a Georgia accent I hear?"

That surprised me a little. I still had an accent, but had lost quite a bit of it in the years I'd been away. "It is. Southern Georgia. And I do live here. I just took it as a summer gig a few years ago, but I fell in love with it. Since I'm a water witch and I hate the cold, it's the perfect place for me. I can't imagine doing anything else."

She tilted her head. "You know, that may not be a bad idea. Are y'all hirin'? I need a job, I need a place to stay, and it's nice to be able to go out in the sun and to talk to somebody without the distraction of thinkin' how they'd taste with crackers."

I laughed. "We're always hiring somewhere on the resort, but take your month and think about what you want to do before you make any decisions."

"Sounds good," she said as she slipped into the pool. "Look, only here one day, and I already have an option."

"Options are always a good thing," I said, following suit. It was rare to hang out with somebody who didn't work at the resort, and I found myself enjoying the rest of the afternoon talking to her and getting to know her.

Turns out, it was lucky for her that I did, because Marissa was about to need somebody in her corner.

<u>Keep reading ...</u>[1]

---

1.   https://books2read.com/u/mBQYnk

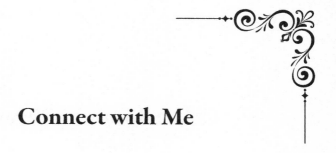

Connect with Me

J oin my readers club here[1] to be the first to hear about new releases, giveaways, contests, and special deals. I'm a reader too, so if I come across a good deal by a great author, I may share in the weekly update, but I won't spam you with salesy BS. I may include obscure trivia, though; you'd be amazed what I learn while researching!

If you're not an email-list person, keep track of new releases by following me:

ON BookBub[2]

On Facebook[3]

On Amazon[4]

Or at Teganmaher.com

Email me – I always love hearing thoughts and feedback, or just drop me a line to say hi!

Happy Reading, and thank you for your time. ☺

---

1. http://eepurl.com/c0MFc5

2. https://www.bookbub.com/authors/tegan-maher

3.   https://www.facebook.com/AuthorTeganMaher/

4.   https://www.amazon.com/Tegan-Maher/e/B0759XYYZD/

Other Books by Tegan Maher

Witches of Keyhole Lake Series

Book 1: Sweet Murder[1]
Book 2: Murder to the Max[2]
Book 4: Mayhem and Murder[3]
Book 5: Murder and Marinade[4]
Book 6: Hook, Line, and Murder[5]
Book 7: Murder of the Month[6]

Witches of Keyhole Lake Shorts

Bubble, Bubble, Here Comes Trouble[7]
Witching for a Miracle[8]
Moonshine Valentine[9]

---

1. https://www.amazon.com/Sweet-Murder-Witches-Keyhole-Mysteries-ebook/dp/B075BR5L45/

2. https://www.amazon.com/Murder-Max-Witches-Keyhole-Mysteries-ebook/dp/B076RT73W7/

3. http://www.amazon.com/Mayhem-Murder-Witches-Keyhole-Mysteries-ebook/dp/B078P9D318

4. https://www.amazon.com/Murder-Marinade-Witches-Keyhole-Mysteries-ebook/dp/B079GB3L4B/

5. https://www.amazon.com/Hook-Line-Murder-Witches-Mysteries-ebook/dp/B07B6QR17H

6. https://www.amazon.com/Murder-Month-Witches-Keyhole-Mysteries-ebook/dp/B07DB33Q8H

7. https://www.amazon.com/Bubble-Here-Comes-Trouble-Witches-ebook/dp/B0782X67ZC/
   ref=la_B0759XYYZD_1_7?s=books&ie=UTF8&qid=1518635101&sr=1-7

8. https://www.amazon.com/Witching-Miracle-Witches-Keyhole-Mysteries-ebook/dp/B079VKXD9P/
   ref=la_B0759XYYZD_1_12?s=books&ie=UTF8&qid=1526530253&sr=1-12

9. https://www.amazon.com/Moonshine-Valentine-Witches-Keyhole-Mysteries-ebook/dp/B07C89K8TY

Cori Sloane Witchy Werewolf Mysteries

Howling for Revenge[10]
Dead Man's Hand[11]

Enchanted Coast Magical Mystery Series

Deadly Daiquiri[12]
Surfboard Slaying[13]
The Purloined Pelt

---

10. https://www.amazon.com/Howling-Revenge-Werewolf-Mystery-Mysteries-ebook/dp/B079R911ZW/

11. https://www.amazon.com/Dead-Mans-Hand-Werewolf-Mysteries-ebook/dp/B07C7KKF8W

12. https://www.amazon.com/Deadly-Daiquiri-Enchanted-Magical-Mystery-ebook/dp/B07CBCY1LQ

13. https://www.amazon.com/dp/B07DF5KCH3

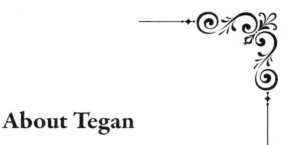

About Tegan

I was born and raised in the South and even hung my motorcycle helmet in Colorado for a few months. I've always had a touch of wanderlust and have never feared just packing up and going on new adventures, whether in real life or via the pages of a great book.

When I was a little girl, I didn't want to grow up to be a writer—I wanted to raise unicorns and be a superhero. When those gigs fell through, I chose the next best thing: creating my own magical lands filled with adventure, magic, humor, and romance.

I live in Florida with my two dogs. When I'm not writing or reading, I'm racing motorcycles or binge-watching anything magical on Netflix.

I'm eternally grateful for all the people who help make my life what is today - friends, readers, family. No woman is an island.